Lock Down Publications and Ca$h
Presents

I0637477

The Daughter
of a
Cartel Boss 2
Legacy Of Death

Written By
SAYNOMORE

SAYNOMORE

First Edition 2025

Printed in the United States of America

Lock Down Publications
P.O. Box 944
Stockbridge, GA 30281
www.lockdownpublications.com

Like our page on Facebook: Lock Down Publications
www.facebook.com/lockdownpublications.ldp

Stay Connected with Us!

Text **LOCKDOWN** to 22828 to stay up-to-date with new releases, sneak peaks, contests and more…

Like our page on Facebook:
Lock Down Publications

Join Lock Down Publications/The New Era Reading Group

Visit our website:
www.lockdownpublications.com

Follow us on Instagram:
Lock Down Publications

Email Us: We want to hear from you!

Chapter 1

The Water Never Lies

The black Cadillac Escalade crept through the fog like a predator, engine purring low, tires whispering over the rain-slicked pavement. Its windows were pitch black, reflecting nothing but the pale glint of the waterfront lights. When it stopped near the edge of Pier 17, the silence that followed was unnaturally still—like the city itself was holding its breath.

A rear door opened with mechanical precision.

She stepped out.

Porscha.

Five-foot-ten in black Louboutin heels that struck the ground like gunshots. Her trench coat clung to her sculpted figure, dark as oil and smooth as silk. The wind lifted her hair just enough to show the diamond-studded dagger tattoo inked behind her left ear—a whisper of her bloodline. Her eyes, shielded behind dark Versace shades, scanned the yacht docked ahead like she was reading its secrets.

She didn't speak. She didn't need to.

Two men in all-black suits flanked her from the vehicle, moving like trained shadows. No greetings. No names. Just loyalty.

The yacht—a white beast named La Sombra—rocked gently, its interior lights casting soft gold through smoked-glass windows. It wasn't just a vessel—it was a floating war room.

Trayvon was waiting.

Her father. Her boss. The architect behind one of the East Coast's most sophisticated laundering empires—masked as a chain of exclusive nightclubs, high-rise condos, and shell nonprofits. A man who shook hands with cartel kings in Tulum and smoked cigars with congressmen in D.C.

Porscha boarded alone.

Inside, the smell of sea salt mixed with Cuban tobacco and quiet power. Trayvon sat in a leather armchair, dressed in a black turtleneck and gold watch that cost more than most funeral plots. He didn't rise.

"Punctual. I raised you right," he said, voice low like a jazz bassline.

Porscha slid off her shades and looked him dead in the eyes.

"You called," she said. "Talk."

Trayvon gestured toward the crystal decanter. Bourbon, neat. No ice.

She didn't sit. Just stared.

"I need someone eliminated," he said flatly. "And I need it clean."

Porscha's eyebrow barely lifted. "Who?"

"Cedric Harper."

She exhaled slowly. The name was poison in the air.

"He's running for mayor," Trayvon continued, "and he's backed by the Gambino boys. He's not one of us, but he's close. Too close."

"And the current mayor?"

"Bought and paid for," Trayvon said, a smirk dancing at the corner of his lips. "Mayor Rapkim gave us the greenlight. And said it's time to tie up loose ends before the campaign gets bloody."

Porscha walked to the window, watching the water slap against the hull. The city lights behind her shimmered like dying stars.

"I'll make it look like a message," she said coldly.

Trayvon leaned back, pleased. "Good girl."

But she didn't turn around. Her mind was already plotting.

Harper wouldn't just die—he would vanish.

No body. No noise. No trace.

Because Porscha wasn't an assassin.

She was the storm that erased everything in her path.

Chapter 2

The bar was dim, the kind of place where conversations died in ashtrays and the jukebox hadn't worked in years. The smell of stale beer and old secrets hung thick in the air. Cigarette smoke lingered like ghosts of men who'd made deals in this very spot and were now rotting in the ground—or worse, living in fear.

Pauly stood at the bar, silent, staring through the back of the bartender's head. His thick fingers curled around two glasses of gin on ice. He didn't drink tonight—not because he was sober, but because he needed clarity. Precision.

The ice cracked in the glass as he turned, slow and deliberate, and made his way toward the back booth. Leather creaked under weight and memory.

Cedric Harper was already sitting there—alone, just like Pauly wanted him. A man wearing power like an expensive coat, thinking he could outrun the past. But Pauly knew the truth.

Nobody escapes the blood they're born into.

Pauly set the drinks down hard. The glasses clinked against the table with the kind of weight that made Cedric raise his eyes. No smile. No words yet. Just that look—sharp, unreadable, and cold as the gin.

Pauly slid into the booth across from him.

"Drink," he said flatly.

Cedric took one look at the glass, then at his cousin. "Since when do you play bartender?"

Pauly's jaw twitched. He didn't laugh. He didn't blink. "Since you started pretending you were anything but a fucking Gambino."

A slow exhale slipped through Cedric's nose as he picked up the glass. He took a sip—not because he wanted to, but because refusing would've been worse.

"You called this meeting," Cedric said, leaning back. "So, get to it. I got places to be."

Pauly leaned forward, his forearms resting on the table like they were loaded cannons.

"I watched your press conference. You looked good. Clean. Ambitious. Almost had me convinced you're the new American dream."

Cedric shrugged, feigning casual. "Perception is power."

Pauly's fingers tapped once on the wood. Then stopped. "Power without loyalty is suicide."

He let that sit. A pause long enough to make Cedric's heartbeat audible.

"You forgot who paved the way for that campaign stage, cousin," Pauly continued, his voice low and venom laced. "It wasn't the voters. It wasn't your bullshit degree from NYU. It was my father. It was my uncle. It was the fucking bones buried under this city that our name put there."

Cedric didn't flinch. But the sweat starting to bead at his temple betrayed him.

"I didn't forget," he replied coolly. "I outgrew it."

Pauly's face darkened. He leaned in so close Cedric could smell the steel in his breath—like gunmetal and fire.

"Outgrew it?" he repeated. "You think you outgrow this? This blood? You're just wearing a different suit to the same funeral, Cedric. You think because you're running for mayor, you're untouchable? You're not even insulated. You're exposed. You're soft."

Cedric sat forward now, his voice sharp. "You done trying to scare me? Because you don't run shit anymore. You're old muscle. A memory. I'm the future."

Pauly chuckled once. It was cruel and joyless.

He reached into his coat pocket and placed something on the table, a single .45 caliber bullet. Unfired. Polished. Whispering promises.

"That bullet's got your name on it," Pauly said, eyes locked. "But I ain't here to pull the trigger. Not yet."

Cedric stared at it.

"Then why the show?"

"Because I want you to remember who you are before someone else reminds you with less mercy."

The ice in Cedric's glass cracked.

Pauly stood up, towering now, the weight of generations behind his stare. He adjusted his coat slowly, like a man preparing for war—not tonight, but soon.

"Blood makes you family," he said coldly. "But loyalty keeps you breathing."

He turned and walked away, leaving Cedric with two choices—the gin, now warm and bitter, and the bullet, gleaming like prophecy.

Chapter 3

Porscha stepped out of the black-on-black, Rolls Royce Phantom like Judgment Day in heels—Glock 9 gripped tight in her manicured hand. Her long coat flared in the wind like wings stitched from shadows. The warehouse loomed ahead, brick and steel, forgotten by the city but about to become legend in the streets. She walked like a woman with death on her mind—slow, deliberate, unbothered.

Inside, the air reeked of fear and blood.

The runner was already gagged and zip-tied to a rusted steel chair bolted to the floor. One eye was swollen shut. His lip was split. Blood ran down his chin in trembling streaks. Two of her soldiers—Rome and Kilo—stood on either side like statues. They'd softened him up. Porscha came to finish him.

She didn't say a word at first. Just stepped forward and stared.

The silence was heavy—funeral heavy.

Click.

She pulled the slide back on the Glock, chambering a round slow enough for him to hear it.

Then she spoke. Calm. Smooth. Deadly.

"You breathe right now because I let you," she said, her voice ice dipped in venom. "That shit in your chest? That's not a heart—it's a time bomb."

She squatted down to eye level. The runner's head trembled.

"You stole from my father. You disappeared with cartel money like this shit was petty theft. Like we don't burn empires over crumbs."

She stood up, pacing.

"Nah. See, you made it personal. You didn't just run off with money, you ran off with our name. That's blasphemy. And I'm the high priestess of consequences."

She snapped her fingers. Rome ripped the gag off. The runner screamed as torn skin came with it.

"Please, Porscha, please—I got kids—"

She pistol-whipped him. Crack! The sound echoed through the hollow space like a firework. A tooth flew from his mouth.

"You got kids?" she laughed, not out of joy, but disgust. "Then you should've taught them what happens when daddy fucks with wolves."

He sobbed. She leaned in closely, dragging the barrel of the Glock across his cheek like a lover.

"You think you're the first rat I've skinned?" she whispered. "I buried snitches so deep the devil pays me rent."

Then, without a blink, she fired a bullet that went through his left kneecap. Bone and flesh exploded. He shrieked like an animal. Blood sprayed across the floor, warm and fast.

Porscha didn't flinch. She looked down at the mess and sighed.

"You bleed real fast for someone who thought he could outrun fate."

He gasped, trying to talk. "It was—just—I was scared— they said they'd kill me—"

She slapped him again, harder.

"And now I will. But I'm gonna make it hurt."

She motioned to Kilo. He handed her a black velvet pouch.

She unzipped it.

Inside, a scalpel. A blowtorch. A set of pliers. A cigar cutter.

The runner's eyes widened with horror.

"Let me paint you a picture," she said, voice now like silk sliding across a razor. "I cut off fingers for every lie. Then I carve my name in your chest—P.O.R.S.C.H.A. Seven letters. Seven slices. Then, if you still got a tongue to talk, I shove it in your mouth and make you chew it."

He started convulsing.

"Talk. Now."

"S-Steinway and 145th!" he blurted. "Backroom— bodega—it's under the goddamn floor—please Porscha, I swear on my kids—"

She paused, watching him shake.

Then she took the pliers—and yanked out one of his teeth anyway.

"You ain't bleeding enough."

He screamed until his voice cracked, until blood sprayed from his lips like spit.

"I believe you," she said coolly. "But this ain't about truth. This is about the price."

She stood up, wiped her gloved hands on a towel, and nodded to her men.

"Leave him. Burn the whole spot. Let this bitch's ashes blow through Brooklyn like a warning."

Rome lit the Molotov. Flames began to creep up the back wall as Kilo poured gas across the floor. The runner thrashed and howled, fire reflecting in his terrified eyes.

Porscha walked back toward the Rolls without looking back. Her heels clicked with calm certainty over the chaos behind her.

She slid into the back seat, leaned back against butter-soft leather, and rolled the tinted window halfway down.

Then she whispered, like a prophecy to the night, "Murder ain't what I do. It's who I am."

The door shut.

And the Rolls disappeared into the shadows like a hearse.

***

Escobar Sanchez was on the private jet. The Gulfstream G650 cut through the clouds like a dagger, thirty-five thousand feet above the chaos he controlled. Inside, the jet's interior gleamed with quiet power—mahogany panels, cream leather seats, gold-plated fixtures. But there was nothing luxurious about the tension that lingered in the air. He sat in the main cabin, sipping dark espresso from a porcelain cup rimmed in gold. No sugar. No milk. Just black, bitter, and boiling—like the man himself.

The silence was heavy, broken only by the low hum of the engines and the occasional rattle of turbulence. Mr. Wright— his sharp-suited consigliere—sat across from him, laptop open, documents displayed, eyes sharp behind gold-framed glasses.

Sanchez leaned back slowly, fingers drumming on the wood grain armrest. He wore a white linen suit so clean it looked ironed by angels, but the expression on his face was carved from stone.

"They think I'm distracted," Sanchez said in low Spanish, his voice smooth but dangerous. "They think because I'm up here, I'm blind to what's happening down there."

He turned his gaze out the window, watching clouds roll like smoke over the world below.

"Porscha is smart. Her father is careful. But even smart people get greedy. And careful people get tired."

Mr. Wright didn't respond. He knew better than to interrupt the storm while it was still gathering.

"They're moving money too fast. Too many eyes. The FBI, DEA—they don't sleep anymore. Every dollar we wash through New York has to be perfect. But they're getting sloppy." Escobar's jaw tightened. "I don't pay for sloppy."

Mr. Wright nodded slowly. "I've already flagged five transactions that don't add up. Porscha's operation moved ninety million in two weeks. That's cartel war numbers."

Escobar smirked.

"Ninety million? That girl's trying to impress me—or bury herself in my books."

He set the espresso cup down with a quiet click.

"She reminds me of her father. Trayvon was a killer before he was a businessman. He understood blood before he understood numbers. That's why I trusted him."

A beat passed.

"But this new generation…" Escobar's voice trailed off, darker now. "They want to build empires overnight. But they don't want to bleed for it."

He leaned forward, and locked eyes with Mr. Wright.

"I built this shit out of ashes. I fed it bones. I carved out a kingdom between bullets and borderlines. And now I see vultures circling my money like I'm dead."

Mr. Wright's voice was steady, respectful. "Would you like me to send a warning?"

Escobar shook his head.

"No. I'm going to New York myself. Set foot in that city like Caesar. I want Porscha to see my eyes when I ask her one question…"

He stood up, fixing the gold cufflink on his wrist.

"Is she loyal—or is she ready to die?"

The jet dipped slightly, turbulence shaking the cabin for a moment.

Sanchez didn't blink.

"Tell my pilot to prepare for wheels down in Teterboro. I want every rat, every banker, every politician we own waiting on my call. And find Trayvon. If Porscha is going rogue, I want to know if it runs in the blood."

Mr. Wright stood, already dialing.

"Yes, Patrón."

Escobar Sanchez turned to the window again, eyes sharp as razors, voice now a whisper, "If they've forgotten who I am... I'll remind them."

***

The private jet pulled into the hanger where there was a black-on-black Cadillac Escalade waiting. That's when the back door opened and Trayvon stepped out of the SUV, looking like a true boss. He made his way over to the private jet as he walked to the steps through the doors.

Trayvon stepped into the room, tailored in a charcoal Tom Ford suit, Rolex iced, eyes calm but alert. He'd been summoned—not requested. And when Escobar Sanchez summoned you, you showed up ready for war, even if it was a conversation.

Escobar sat back, a fresh glass of aged tequila in hand. His eyes narrowed as Trayvon entered. Not a smile. Not a word.

Trayvon gave a small nod and took a seat across from him, legs spread, elbows resting on his knees.

"Appreciate the ride," he said coolly.

Escobar studied him like a vulture deciding whether the body was still warm.

"I don't offer rides. I offer chances."

A long pause.

"I hear the city's moving faster than my money," Escobar continued. "Too fast. Too loud. I smell ambition."

Trayvon met his gaze, unflinching. "You smell growth."

Escobar leaned forward. "I smell heat, old friend. Investigations. Wire taps. Anonymous tips. Bank accounts bouncing like rubber balls in a burning building. I smell the kind of shit that lands people like me in a federal box underground. So, tell me, Trayvon—do I have a problem in New York?"

Trayvon clasped his hands together, his voice steady, deliberate. "No. You don't have a problem. You have the city in a headlock."

He leaned in, matching Escobar's intensity.

"The mayor's in our pocket. The DA's chasing ghosts. The police department's chasing its own damn tail. And every political player that matters is eating off our plate—even if they don't know it."

Escobar raised a brow. "And Porscha?"

Trayvon's jaw tightened. His daughter's name carried weight.

"She's doing what you taught us all to do—rule with fear before love. She ain't going rogue. She's going ruthless."

Escobar said nothing, waiting.

"She's making them believe, Escobar," Trayvon continued. "Believe that the cartel ain't just numbers and cash. It's a presence. It's death in heels. It's a whisper that makes grown men piss themselves. That's why they're moving fast—not because she's greedy, because they're scared."

Escobar took a long sip from his glass, never breaking eye contact.

Trayvon's voice grew quieter and heavier.

"You gave us New York to make the city bow. Porscha ain't playing queen. She's playing executioner. You wanted fear? She is fear. But never mistake that for disloyalty. That girl would slit her own throat before she crosses you."

The two men sat in silence. Outside the window, the lights of Manhattan sparkled in the distance, like a kingdom they both owned.

Escobar finally leaned back, swirling the tequila in his glass.

"I remember stories you told me when she was a little girl... hiding behind your leg listening to you as you did business. Eyes sharp even then. Like a jaguar cub."

Trayvon smirked. "She ain't hiding no more."

Escobar chuckled low and dark.

"No, she's not. And that scares me more than it comforts me."

He stood, walked to the bar, poured a second glass, and handed it to Trayvon.

"Here's to daughters who make men kneel."

Trayvon raised his glass. "And fathers who make killers out of angels."

They drank.

But the silence that followed wasn't peace—it was an understanding. Two empires. One throne. One daughter caught in the crossfire between legacy and loyalty.

Escobar placed his glass down.

"Tell her I'm watching."

Trayvon nodded. "She already knows."

Chapter 4

The Montauk night was quiet. Too quiet.

Cedric Harper's brother, Dorian, and his wife Melanie had just settled in for the evening. A fire cracked in the living room. Wine glasses half-full on the marble kitchen island. Jazz whispering from the ceiling speakers. The kind of life only the connected could afford.

Then came the knock.

One soft tap. Then two harder ones. A rhythm too precise to be random.

Dorian went to answer it, annoyed, barefoot in his slacks. When he opened the door, he didn't even get a full gasp before Rakim's silenced pistol was shoved into his chest.

"Inside," Rakim growled, stepping in like death in human skin.

Behind him came Porscha, dressed in a sleek, black leather trench coat, not a hair out of place. And Corey, stone-faced, carrying a black duffel bag heavy with evil intent.

Melanie screamed.

The silence was shattered.

"What the f—" Dorian started, before Rakim pistol-whipped him across the mouth. Blood sprayed across the white oak floors. His knees buckled, and he dropped like a paper doll.

Porscha walked in like a queen visiting a slum. Calm. Cold. Her heels tapped with sovereign authority.

"Where is your brother, Dorian?" she asked, voice smooth as a scalpel.

Dorian coughed, spitting blood. "I don't know."

Porscha didn't blink. She motioned to Corey. He zipped open the duffel and pulled out a heavy-duty roll of plastic sheeting, duct tape, and a black tarp.

"You know," Porscha said, "I always wondered how far blood can spread on white floors."

Melanie tried to run. Rakim grabbed her by the hair, slamming her face into the wall so hard the drywall cracked. She crumpled to the ground, whimpering.

"Don't!" Dorian yelled. "She doesn't know anything! Please!"

"Oh, I believe that," Porscha said, crouching down in front of Melanie. "But pain has a funny way of making people talk, even if they think they don't know nothing."

They dragged them both into the kitchen, wrapping the floor in plastic. Chairs were zip-tied. A stainless-steel bucket was filled in the sink.

"Start with her," Porscha said, sitting at the island like she was about to be served wine.

Corey held Melanie's face steady. Rakim dumped the first splash of water over the towel covering her mouth and nose.

Melanie screamed beneath the fabric—a muffled, drowning shriek—her body convulsing, tied tight.

"No! Please!" Dorian begged, struggling, tears running hot. "I swear to God—"

"Wrong name to swear to," Porscha cut in. "I'm God here. This city? It's my fucking heaven."

Another bucket. Another scream. Melanie gagged and gasped between sobs.

Porscha stood, heels echoing off the walls as she walked slowly to Dorian.

"You think the mafia runs New York?" she whispered in his ear. "You think your little Italian brother with his mob ties scares me? I send mayors to lunch with demons. I got judges laundering my money in donation envelopes. I make cartel bosses kneel to me."

She pulled his head back and stared into his soul.

"When I say I want a name, you better pray to me…not for her, but for yourself."

"I don't know where he is!" Dorian screamed. "I haven't seen him in weeks!"

Porscha smiled. Then backed away. Snapped her fingers.

Rakim pulled out two large plastic bags and slipped one over Melanie's face, duct-taping it tight around her neck.

The screams turned into a choking, desperate moan.

"Stop! Stop!" Dorian sobbed.

"You know what I hate?" Porscha said, circling back toward him. "Lies. And men who let women die for their cowardice."

Then came his turn.

The second bag slipped over Dorian's face, his eyes widened, bulging, veins popping in his forehead as he thrashed. His body knocked the chair to the floor. He writhed, his legs spasming.

Melanie's body went still.

Dorian saw it—his wife's last, trembling twitch—and then he knew.

"You could've given me a name," Porscha said, kneeling beside him as he slowly suffocated. "Now all you'll give me is silence."

His movements slowed.

His final, rattled groan echoed in the bloody quiet of the house.

Dead.

Porscha stood alone now. Her coat was untouched by the blood sprayed across the room like an abstract painting.

"Leave 'em. Make sure the cops find 'em just like this," she told Rakim and Corey. "I want them to know this wasn't a robbery. This was judgment."

Rakim nodded, pulling out a burner phone and dropping it beside the corpse with a picture of Cedric Harper's campaign poster on the screen.

Porscha looked around the room, the floor soaked in blood and the plastic crinkled under two corpses.

"When the feds and detectives get here," she said, walking out with death in her stride, "they'll realize they're not chasing a suspect. They're chasing a fucking phantom."

***

Trayvon leaned back in the leather booth tucked deep in the private corner of La Sirena, an upscale Italian restaurant in Midtown Manhattan, known for keeping secrets hotter than its marinara. Candlelight flickered across the glass of bourbon in front of him, untouched. He didn't drink during business—especially not this kind. The atmosphere was elegant, but the air was weighted, thick with something unspoken.

Across from him sat Mr. Wright—Escobar Sanchez's personal attorney. Dressed immaculately in a midnight-blue suit, no tie, top button fastened tight like his loyalty. Calm, calculating, dead behind the eyes. He looked like a Wall Street executive but smelled like blood money.

"Trayvon," Mr. Wright began, his voice like silk over a razor's edge. "We both know why I'm here. Escobar doesn't send me unless the matter is critical. And he doesn't tolerate loose threads. Not in his business, not in his legacy."

Trayvon adjusted his cufflinks slowly. "I know what this is. And I ain't new to it. But if Escobar think I'm about to jump at shadows, he's mistaken."

Mr. Wright smirked. "That's just it—there are no shadows anymore. It's daylight. Clean daylight. The war down south? It's real. Families—whole bloodlines—are getting erased. Escobar needs clean money, now. Hundreds of millions. Washed thoroughly. No fumbles. No 'almosts.' This isn't a suggestion."

He leaned forward, voice low. "He's already killed men, women, children. Anyone with the wrong last name. This isn't about fear, it's about precision. He trusts you, Trayvon."

The silence settled between them like dust over a sealed grave.

Trayvon leaned back in the leather chair, eyes half-lidded, elbows on the armrests like a judge waiting on testimony. Mr. Wright didn't blink. He merely opened the slim folio resting beside his espresso, slid a thin stack of papers forward, and rotated them toward Trayvon.

"Fourteen shell entities," Mr. Wright said, voice smooth as graphite. "Two in the Caymans. One in Cyprus. The rest distributed across domestic fronts—New York, Atlanta, Vegas, Miami. You'll notice the banks are compliant. The routing is tight. Swiss and Israeli corridors, no U.S. flags raised unless someone's actively looking."

Trayvon didn't touch the papers. He let the words hang there.

"And if someone is looking?" Trayvon asked. His voice didn't carry concern—just logistics.

Mr. Wright folded his hands. "Then they're not doing it legally. This paperwork is built for passive audits, not federal investigations. You'll have five months of runway, minimum. After that, our sources inside the Treasury will shift the burden."

Trayvon nodded, slow. "And Escobar?"

Mr. Wright's mouth curled slightly. "Escobar isn't interested in micromanaging. He's delegating. New York is yours. The volume—he expects you to handle it. Quietly. Cleanly. Without drawing blood or headlines."

Trayvon finally picked up the first page. Skimmed. He wasn't a lawyer, but he could read structure. Each LLC was a door—behind it, a vault. They'd been engineered to blend in with the city's real estate shadows—a construction firm in Brooklyn, a seafood distributor in the Bronx, two digital advertising shells in Midtown.

"How much are we moving?" Trayvon asked, not looking up.

Mr. Wright didn't blink. "Initial injection—seventy-five million. Recurring monthly flow—twenty to twenty-five million. Spikes during Q3 and Q4, depending on product movement out of Juárez."

Trayvon's fingers paused. "That's cartel war season."

"Exactly. Which means blood down there. But up here?" Mr. Wright gestured lightly to the glass skyline behind him. "We keep it clean. Your daughter oversees the Midtown LLCs. You handle distribution. Escobar wants this to look like a Wall Street portfolio—not a body count."

Trayvon exhaled slowly. "She's not gonna like you assigning her."

Mr. Wright shrugged. "I'm not assigning her. You are."

Another silence.

"I need guarantees," Trayvon said finally. "If this goes sideways, it's my name on the paper. Not Escobar's."

Mr. Wright leaned forward. For the first time, his smile disappeared.

"You're not asking for guarantees. You're asking for protection. And Trayvon… protection is earned. Not promised."

Trayvon held the stare. He didn't flinch, but he felt the weight of that sentence land like a coffin lid.

Mr. Wright adjusted his cufflinks, then tapped a small business card forward. White. Embossed. Minimalist.

"Call that number. Burn the phone after. It routes through a rotating exchange in Medellín. If you ever feel compromised… speak one word, 'Atlas.' You'll have thirty-six hours of silence to clean up or disappear."

Trayvon took the card.

Mr. Wright stood. The meeting was over.

"Welcome to the other side of the city, Mr. Ward."

He walked out without waiting for a handshake.

***

Rain taps the panoramic glass like a ticking clock. Up here, in the private suite of Horizon Legacy, Porscha and Trayvon sit above the city like gods playing chess with kings. The air is rich with truffle oil, saffron butter, and old power.

Trayvon, calm and cold, cuts into a medium-rare ribeye, then wipes the blade clean like a man used to blood on his hands.

"Escobar wants us to clean five hundred million."

He doesn't flinch when he says it, just pours two glasses of Ace of Spades. Slides one to his daughter.

Porscha, in matte black silk, doesn't move right away. Then she leans forward, lips twisted with disbelief.

"After everything we did for that motherfucker?"

Trayvon just lifts his glass.

"Talk to me."

Porscha's voice is razor-sharp now. Her eyes lit with heat.

"We kidnapped a federal judge's family, Tray. You remember that? Four bodies deep to pull that off without a sound. Took the DA's people the same night. We made the city bleed silence just so Sanchez's son could walk out the back of that courtroom like a damn ghost."

Trayvon nods once. Calm. That assassin calm.

"And don't forget the fed…"

"I ain't," she snaps. "We executed a federal agent in broad daylight. That FBI undercover who flagged Sanchez's son at the restaurant and got him out of jail before the prints hit the system? Burned his body to the ribs before sun-up. Whole task force was in tears when they pulled his body out the East River."

She leans in now, teeth clenched.

"We erased a federal agent for that man. We went to war with the Mafia for that man. You remember what they did to Calico? What they did to Nina's little brother?"

"They dumped that boy in the Hudson with no eyes," Trayvon says softly. "I remember."

Silence hovers, heavy with ghosts.

"And we still hit back," Porscha says. "Still smoked four of their lieutenants. Two restaurant owners. Car-bombed a capo and his wife in Brooklyn. We bled for that alliance. Bled to keep Escobar's name out of headlines."

Trayvon sips slow his eyes burning with pride.

"That's why he came to us. Nobody else got that reach. Nobody else got that fear."

"And now he wants his dirty half-billion cleaned like it's nothing?"

"Like it's a favor," Trayvon murmurs. "No offer. No cut. No loyalty."

Porscha's voice drops, lethal calm.

"He forgets who yanked his puppet strings."

Trayvon smirks now—that proud father smirk.

"He thinks he's the storm. But we been the flood."

He sets his glass down and leans in, voice just above the music playing soft from the corner.

"You know why we did all that for him, P? Not outta fear. Not outta friendship. We did it to remind the whole damn underworld who really writes the ending."

"We're not the puppets. We're not the master."

"We're the hands that built the whole damn stage."

Porscha nods slowly, storm in her eyes.

"So, what we doing now?

Trayvon exhales, checks his Rolex.

"We clean it. But on our terms. Our speed. Our numbers. And when the time comes, we cut the power from his empire like lights in a blackout."

She raises her glass.

"And if he flinches?"

"We burn him down. Quiet. Clean. Like he never existed."

They toast in silence, two legends with blood on their hands and power in their veins, sitting above the world they run—one body at a time.

***

The sun had just started to set over the Sanchez estate, casting a gold glow across the manicured lawn and marble terrace. The breeze carried the scent of orange blossoms and gun oil—two things the Sanchez family had always kept close. In the back of the estate, behind tall walls and tighter secrets, Escobar Sanchez sat on the teak deck of his sprawling compound, swirling a glass of aged rum. His white shirt was crisp, open at the collar, gold shining on his wrist and neck, but his expression was cold steel.

Emilio stepped out, fresh from the gym, sweat still on his neck, black tee clinging to his back. He'd been summoned, and when Escobar summoned you, you didn't ask why. You came.

"You wanted to see me?" Emilio asked, standing tall but cautious.

Escobar didn't look at him. Just took a slow sip and finally muttered, "Send five times the usual amount to Trayvon. After that, we stop."

Emilio blinked. Confused. "Stop?"

Escobar finally turned to face him. "That's the last shimmer going north. After this, no more shipments to New York."

Emilio stepped forward, chest rising.

"Why? Why shut off our biggest pipeline? New York's been producing more money than Texas, more than California. Hell, more than Colombia in a good year. That's Trayvon and Porscha's territory. You cut them off and you cut off our future."

Escobar leaned back, slow and deliberate, his gaze never wavering.

"We have more money than we can clean. It's not about stacking anymore, it's about converting. About surviving." Emilio's voice cracked, heat bubbling up.

"Surviving? They saved me. Trayvon got me out of jail before my name came up on Interpol's red list. Porscha got the DA in Queens to drop all charges against me. You weren't even going to move. They did. You made promises to them."

Escobar's eyes darkened, the rum glass clinking softly as he set it down.

"And that promise ends with my word. That debt is paid. You want to honor someone? Honor the family. Honor the cartel. Because right now, we're not at war with New York— we're about to be at war with every rival cartel from Sinaloa to Michoacán. And that is the war that matters."

"But they bled for us," Emilio fired back. "You think I forgot what they did in Brooklyn? In Jersey? That's not business, that was brotherhood."

Escobar rose from his chair slowly, with the weight of a man who'd outlived friends, enemies, and illusions.

"You think Porscha is your sister? You think Trayvon's your father? They played their role, took their payment. Don't confuse survival with sentiment. Don't mistake a deal with devotion."

Emilio shook his head, fists clenched at his sides.

"They risked everything. When Interpol had that warrant on me—for murder, for extortion, for everything—I was facing extradition to Spain, then Mexico. You know what that meant. Torture. Death. They saved me. And now you want me to turn off the tap and walk away like it's just math?"

Escobar moved in close, voice now low and venomous.

"You're alive because I let you be alive. Don't you ever forget that. You think this is about who saved you? I made you. You carry the Sanchez name. And as long as you wear that, you follow my word. We're done with New York. That's not a negotiation. That's an order."

Emilio's jaw tensed. His chest rose with every breath like he was ready to swing. But then… he faltered. Eyes dropped. His pulse slowed.

Escobar stepped back, voice calmer now—almost surgical.

"Trayvon and Porscha made their bed. If they drown, they drown. That's their bridge to cross. We have a real war coming. One that'll wipe us off the map if we don't move right. I don't care about alliances made in prison cells or backroom clubs. I care about the next ten years. About building something I can hand down without it being buried in bodies."

Silence.

The garden was quiet except for the sound of cicadas and distant water running through the fountain. Emilio stood still, fists slowly unclenching.

"I understand," he said at last.

Escobar nodded once, picking up his glass.

"Good. Then don't question me again."

Emilio turned to walk away. Shoulders heavy. Pride cracked. The man who once owed his life to the streets of New York had just been forced to watch that loyalty burn under the boot of bloodline and power.

As he disappeared into the house, Escobar took another sip of his drink and looked out across the horizon.

"This isn't about loyalty. It's about legacy."

***

Dark streets. Neon flickers. The sound of cash machines humming, washers spinning, grills sizzling. New York breathes through its storefronts—and Porscha's about to own its lungs.

Montage
A laundromat in Bed-Stuy.
An older Dominican man shakes his head. "I told you—I can't run no money through here."
Porscha doesn't speak. She nods once.
Outside, a black van rolls up. Two men in ski masks drag him out of the shop ten minutes later. His wife screams.
Two weeks later—same shop, same name, new owner. Porscha's lieutenants count bills in the backroom while the machines spin clean.

A Jamaican jerk spot In Flatbush.
Owner says, "You want to use my kitchen for what? Nah, I got kids, I got family—"
BANG.
One shot. Clean. Cold. His son finds the body in the freezer the next morning.
By nightfall, Porscha's people are running product through the kitchen, money gets vacuum sealed between chicken crates.

A small motel off Queens Boulevard.
The front desk clerk slides over the keys to Room 12. No questions.
The manager who refused to lease rooms for "drops?" He disappeared three days ago. Surveillance footage lost in a power outage.
Now Room 12 stays booked—day and night. So does 14. So does 16.

A corner bodega in The Bronx.
Blood on the floor.
Cashier trembling.
Owner chained in the freezer with his tongue in a Ziploc bag—a message for the next guy who thinks "no" is an answer.

Next week, store's back open. Cleaner than ever. Shelves stocked, front legit, back room all business. Porscha's business.

***

Chief Lawson, sleeves rolled, pacing. Detective Boatwright stares at the board. Red strings, pins. All led to Porscha.

Detective Flowers sat, arms crossed, silent and simmering.

Lawson: "She's not just taking turf—she's replacing entire ecosystems. This isn't a crew, it's a fucking corporation."

Boatwright: "We got twenty-five confirmed flips. Laundromats, restaurants, motels, bodega chains... All within six weeks. Like a goddamn plague."

Flowers: "And not a single soul talking. Every witness either vanished, got paid off, or found Jesus. You walk in those neighborhoods, you feel it—fear with lipstick and red-bottom heels. That's Porscha."

Lawson: "You know what this is? It's 'get down or lay down.' And everybody laid down."

Boatwright: "She killed her way into power... now she's cleaning money while the city looks the other way."

Lawson: "Not the city. The people. And you can't police ghosts."

***

Porscha stands on a rooftop overlooking the East River. Night breeze in her curls. Her lieutenant hands her a folder—twenty-five properties. All signed. All hers.

She lights a cigar, slow drag. Below her, the city churns—clean and dirty, broken and beautiful.

Porscha said, "I didn't steal this city. I inherited it... when y'all stopped protecting it."

10:32 p.m.

Night hung low and heavy over the city, like a velvet curtain soaked in sin. Outside Club Mercedes, bass from inside throbbed through the walls, the line of people at the entrance coiled around the corner—bodies dressed in too little, chasing too much. Neon lights glimmered off polished chrome and the glossy black skin of high-end whips parked curbside. But none of that glitter masked the death riding in silent approach.

Lance was parked two blocks away in the far end of the back lot, tucked in the shadows behind the dumpster wall. Porscha had warned him not to play sloppy when it came to her name, but he was cocky, untouchable—or so he thought. The girl he was with—pretty, brown-skinned, lashes thick and lips fuller than sin—was straddling him in the passenger seat of the matte black Benz coupe, windows fogged up, tension thick. His pistol lay on the floorboard, shirt halfway off, belt undone.

The girl giggled, biting her lip.

"You always fuck with the windows down, huh?"

Lance grinned. "Gotta let God watch."

He never heard the first SUV pull in. Or the second. Twin engines rolled in like predators—blacked-out Tahoes crawling slow, tires crunching gravel, headlights off. Then came the clicks—subtle, soft, chilling—the sound of chambered death.

In less than three seconds, the darkness erupted.

All you heard was the sound of gunshots echoing in the darkness. Twin P90s on full-auto opened fire through all four SUV windows.

Glass exploded in high-definition chaos. The windshield shattered instantly as the first round hit Lance in the throat, shredding muscle and artery in a hot splash of red. He jerked, body going limp before his brain could register pain. The girl screamed—tried to duck—but the second volley tore into her back and spine, severing everything from the waist up.

Blood sprayed the inside of the car like a Jackson Pollock nightmare. Windows burst. Bullets punched through the doors, the roof, the console. Her hand hit the horn, pressing it down in a long, helpless wail as her head slammed the dashboard. Her wig peeled off from the force of impact, sticking to the rearview mirror like some sick souvenir.

More than three hundred rounds tore through the car in under fifteen seconds.

Steel jacketed lead turned flesh into vapor. Plastic melted. Rubber burned. Steam hissed from the radiator. The once-clean Benz now looked like a murder sculpture—doors pocked with bullet holes, blood dripping in rivulets from the side panels, the glass liquified and fused into shards.

The gunfire echoed like thunder down the block.

***

Inside Club Mercedes, the music hiccupped as the bass synced with reality. Bottles froze mid-pour. Dancers paused mid-drop. And Paris, the manager, was the first to run toward the back hallway that led to the lot.

"Turn the fucking music off!" she screamed.

The DJ killed the sound.

Screams replaced it.

A rush of high heels and designer cologne spilled out the fire exit. Paris sprinted ahead, Glock in hand, heart pounding. Her stilettos clapped hard against pavement until she skidded to a stop—mouth wide open, blinking, breathing like she'd been punched in the chest.

The car was unrecognizable. Steam floated like ghost breath above the hood. Inside, Lance's face was gone, his lower jaw blown off, eyes open but empty, head resting at a wrong angle against the backseat. His right arm twitched involuntarily, nerves still firing postmortem. The girl's body lay slumped over the gearshift, ribs showing through torn flesh, blood covering her breasts like war paint. Her teeth were on the dashboard.

Paris didn't scream. She just whispered, "Oh, my fucking God..."

People behind her gagged. One man threw up in the bushes. Another girl fainted.

Two bouncers ran over, guns drawn, but the SUVs were already long gone—vanished into the night like phantoms. No license plates. No tire marks. Just a trail of hot brass casings that glittered under the parking lot lights.

One of the bullets had pierced the trunk and ignited the subwoofer. Smoke hissed upward, turning the scene even more hellish. Paris looked down at her phone, hands shaking, and hit one name—Porscha's.

She didn't wait for a greeting.

"They fucking executed Lance," she breathed. "Outside the club. In the parking lot. They lit his ass up like Fourth of July. He's gone. They dumped over three hundred rounds on him, P."

Silence. Then Porscha's voice came through, calm as an executioner's blade.

"Was it personal?"

Paris swallowed hard. "Two black SUVs. Looked military. P90s. This wasn't random."

Porscha didn't answer immediately. The silence on her end buzzed like a slow-building storm.

"Lock the club down," she finally said. "Nobody in or out. Not even God."

"Y-Yeah. Yeah, I got you."

Paris looked around, her eyes scanning the stunned, frozen crowd now forming a half-circle near the car. Cell phones were already recording. Police would be here in two minutes, media in ten.

But Paris didn't care about any of that.

Because this, this wasn't a hit.

This was a declaration of war.

Chapter 5

Blood

The phone was still warm in her hand when Porscha ended the call with Paris. For ten full seconds she didn't move, didn't blink, didn't breathe.

She was seated in the back of a Maybach, parked in a private lot off West 47th. Quiet jazz played low on the stereo, the kind of music you sipped wine to—not the kind you made death decisions over.

But the moment Paris said the words, "They lit his ass up like Fourth of July," the music meant nothing. The world around her stopped existing.

Lance was gone.

One of her wolves. One of her day-one soldiers. Loyal, brutal, funny-ass Lance—with the dumb grin and fast trigger. A man who bled for her, who once took a bullet meant for her in East New York and laughed about it after.

Now?

Gone. Shredded in a parking lot while his dick was still out.

The rage built from her gut and rose slowly. It wasn't loud or theatrical. Porscha didn't cry. She didn't scream. She didn't throw anything. Her anger was the kind that boiled bones—the kind that made men disappear and made morgues busy.

"Driver," she said coldly.

"Yes, ma'am?"

"Turn that fuckin' music off."

Click.

Silence.

Porscha leaned forward and reached for the sleek touchpad console built into the armrest. She opened a folder labeled Black List. Names. Numbers. Pictures. Every unfinished war was cataloged there. She didn't know who ordered the hit yet—but she had ideas. Maybe it was Escobar trying to flex muscle. Maybe it was Cedric Harper testing her defenses. Or maybe it was some third snake who just made a grave mistake.

She'd find out.

And when she did?

They weren't just going to die.

They were going to suffer.

Her hands shook, but only for a moment. Then she picked up her encrypted phone, dialing through a back-channel system she hadn't touched since Sunday the 15th Wedding Day Massacre.

A voice answered. Raspy. Male. Eastern European accent.

"Speak."

"Activate protocol Ghost Garden," she said flatly.

There was a pause.

"...Are you sure?"

"You heard me. I want surveillance eyes on the city, in The Bronx, Club Mercedes from the past forty-eight hours. Every plate scanned. Every signal pinged. Burn every back door. I want blood, Vasko."

Another pause. Then, "Da. It will be done."

She hung up.

The driver glanced back. "Ms. Porscha... are you alright?"

Her eyes cut to him through the rearview like razors.

"Do I look alright?"

He said nothing more.

Her phone buzzed again—Paris.

"Say it," Porscha answered, voice tight.

"They're taking Lance's body out now. Detectives everywhere. Cameras. Helicopters. They covering it like it's goddamn JFK."

Porscha sucked her teeth and spat it out like venom. "Good. Let the city see it. Let 'em all know what happens next ain't business. It's personal."

Paris hesitated. "You want me to close the club down for the week?"

"No," Porscha said. "Keep it open."

"Open?"

"I want them to think I'm calm," she said. "I want them to believe I'm processing this." Her voice dropped to a whisper soaked in violence. "And when they relax… when they let their fuckin' guard down—I want you to remind them who I am."

Paris exhaled. "Got it."

"Double every shooter on the payroll. Anybody breathes funny near my club, I want their whole lineage in the morgue."

"Yes, ma'am."

The call ended.

Porscha leaned her head back and stared out the window at the New York skyline glowing against the black.

She could feel it—deep in her bones.

This wasn't going to end with a bullet or two. This wasn't going to end with a name getting crossed off quietly.

This was war.

She pulled out a .380 from her ankle holster and stared at it for a long time. Then she pulled out her phone one more time, scrolling to Trayvon.

She hit call.

When he answered, his voice was groggy. "What is it?"

"Lance is dead."

"…What?"

"They ambushed him. Two SUVs. P90s. They lit him the fuck up in the lot outside Mercedes. Left him looking like hamburger meat."

Silence.

"Who did it?" Trayvon asked.

"I don't know yet," she said. "But when I find out?"

"What you need?"

"I need clearance," she said. "Full authority. I'm going scorched earth. I don't give a fuck who dies in the crossfire."

Trayvon was quiet again. Then came a slow sigh.

"You got it."

Click.

Porscha sat back. The city sparkled in the distance like it didn't know it was about to bleed.

And she smiled.

Because now?

Now it was her turn.

***

The Yankees were down by two runs, in the bottom of the seventh. The screen above the bar glowed a soft blue, the only modern light in the joint. A thin haze of cigar smoke curled through the air like a ghost with nowhere to go. Sinatra played low on the jukebox in the corner, the kind of sound that made time feel like it was bleeding backward.

Pauly sat at the far end of the bar, legs crossed, wrist heavy with a gold Cuban link watch that hadn't ticked since '96. His cigar burned steady between two thick fingers, and the crystal glass in front of him held two fingers of eighteen-year Lagavulin.

No one sat too close. No one talked too loudly.

This wasn't the kind of place where drunks got rowdy. This was a temple. A sanctuary for old blood, where murderers drank in peace and memory clung to the walls like dried blood behind fresh paint.

Near the jukebox, Tommy Migs played poker with three of the regulars—ex-union guys and one crooked dockworker with a twitchy eye. At the table by the men's room, Nicky Bricks ran his mouth about old hits like they were baseball cards. Everyone knew not to interrupt Pauly when he was watching the game, especially with that look in his eyes.

He wasn't smiling. But he wasn't angry either.

He was satisfied.

Then, just after a Yankees double sent the crowd at Yankee Stadium into a roar on TV, the door creaked open. Cold air swept in. Heads turned. Two black-clad men walked in—Rocco and Marcelli. Their jackets still smelled like exhaust and their boots carried the dirt of Queens.

Pauly didn't look away from the screen.

"You boys took your time," he muttered.

Rocco grinned, nodding as he slid onto the stool beside him. "We wanted it clean. No survivors. No screams. Just metal and smoke."

Marcelli leaned in close. "She got the message, boss."

Pauly finally looked over.

"You see her face?"

"No," Rocco said. "But Paris came out screaming. It was bad, boss. They didn't just die. They got butchered."

Pauly puffed slowly on his cigar, eyes calm.

"Good."

He looked back up at the screen—another out. Yankees still trailing.

He took a sip of whiskey and let the silence build around him. The bar had quieted like a church mid-sermon.

He didn't have to say it out loud, but it hung in the air between them anyway.

This was retribution, for the Sunday the 15th Wedding Day Massacre.

It had been five years since that day in Central Park. Sun was shining. Kids were throwing rice. The bride wore white, and Vince Calabrese—his friend, his fuckin' brother—stood under an arbor with tears in his eyes.

That was before the black SUVs rolled up.

Before Porscha's men opened fire with .223s and scoped ARs. Before fifteen people hit the grass in a pool of brains and wedding cake.

His niece's veil was blown off her head by gunfire.

The bride bled out in her mother's arms. Vince's face was unrecognizable. It was supposed to be sacred. A day of love. Porscha made it into war.

And Pauly had waited. Waited with the patience of a wolf in winter.

Now?

Now the first card had been played.

Rocco lit his own cigarette. "You sure you don't wanna lay low?"

Pauly smirked. "For what?"

"Porscha ain't gonna take this lightly."

Pauly chuckled.

"That's the fuckin' point. I don't want her calm. I want her emotional. Reactive. She's dangerous when she's focused—but sloppy when she's grieving. She's gonna lash out. She's gonna come for blood. And when she does..."

He looked at them both with eyes like granite.

"...I'll bury her."

Another crack of the bat from the TV—double play. End of the inning.

Pauly raised his glass, toasted the screen, and took another sip.

"Now shut the fuck up and let me watch the game."

And just like that, the bar went back to low murmurs and Sinatra.

But something had shifted.

The war had started.

And Pauly?

He was just getting comfortable.

***

The living room was dark except for the flickering light of the TV, muted, cycling through static on a local news channel. Cedric Harper sat on the edge of a leather armchair, shirt half-buttoned, tie hanging loose like a noose around his neck. A half-empty bottle of bourbon sweated on the coffee table in front of him, next to a crystal glass he hadn't bothered to refill in over an hour.

He was drunk. Not the sloppy kind—the hollow kind. The kind of drunk that came with grief that sat heavy in the chest like a loaded pistol.

His eyes were red. Not just from the liquor.

"They killed him… because of me," he muttered, slurring slightly, talking to no one and everyone. "Because I opened that fuckin' door again…"

His fingers trembled as he reached for the glass, staring through it like it held answers. The ice had melted. The drink was watered down—weak. Unlike his brother. Unlike Marcus.

"He was just tryin' to live clean… You didn't ask for none of this," Cedric whispered, eyes glossed over, jaw clenched. "You had a wife. A family. And they took that from you— because I couldn't stay out of the game."

He slammed the glass down. Hard. Not enough to shatter, but enough to crack it. A single tear rolled down his cheek, but he didn't wipe it. He just sat there—bleeding inside.

"They came for me… and they used you to do it."

He stood up suddenly, pacing, fingers raking through his hair, body swaying from liquor and rage. His voice rose— not to yell, but to scream into silence.

"I'm sorry, man! I'm so fuckin' sorry!" he cried. "You didn't deserve that! Not like that… not like that."

The weight in his chest turned into something darker. Something sharp.

"They think I'm gonna just sit back? Huh?" he hissed, staring at a framed photo of his brother on the mantle. "They think I'm just gonna weep and move on?"

He picked up the picture—his hand shaking—and held it to his chest.

"I swear to God, Marcus... I'm gonna burn every last one of them for this."

He looked into the photo like he was looking for his brother's forgiveness. But all he saw was what he lost.

***

The city skyline glowed behind the tall glass windows of Rakim's office. Dim lights. Heavy air. A bottle of Hennessy sat open on the table. Porscha's second-in-command—a shadow-faced man named Renzo, sharp suit, cold eyes—stood quietly in the corner, arms crossed, waiting for orders.

Rakim's phone buzzed. Unknown number. He answered with a tired edge in his voice.

Rakim: "Talk."

Distorted Voice: "You want to know who carved Lance up in that parking lot?"

Rakim sat forward, eyes narrowing. Renzo looked up, catching the shift in his energy.

Rakim: "Who the fuck is this?"

Voice: "Someone who hears things... someone who knows where the bodies are buried. You want answers, it's gonna cost you."

Rakim: "How much?"

Voice: "Fifty racks. And I don't do names over the phone. You meet me—in person. Neutral ground. You come alone."

Rakim's jaw flexed. "You realize who you're callin', right? I don't pay ghosts."

Voice: "Then stay blind. But your little assassin queen? She just made enemies that don't play fair. You want who pulled the strings, you bring the money."

Silence.

Rakim: "Location?"

Voice: "You'll get it an hour before. No names. No tricks. You'll get what you pay for."

Click.

The line went dead. Rakim stared at the phone, then glanced at Renzo.

Rakim: "Get the cash. Porscha's gonna want blood. I need names first."

Chapter 6

The room smelled of old leather, burnt tobacco, and regret. The blinds were drawn, the fireplace flickered low, and a bottle of scotch sat untouched beside a half-filled glass. Big Pete—once a feared name in the Five Families—sat slouched in a cracked recliner, puffing slowly on a thick cigar. His once-slick black hair was graying at the edges, and his eyes were tired, but alert.

He didn't flinch when the door opened.

Agent Stallone, dressed in a plain black windbreaker and jeans, stepped in slowly, clipboard in hand.

Stallone: "You think about how this ends, Pete?"

Pete scoffed, the smoke curling from his lips like a ghost escaping a tomb.

Big Pete: "How it ends? Hell, I didn't even think I'd be here tellin' on people I swore blood to. I was a fuckin' don. Now look at me—hiding in some shithole cabin, labeled a rat. Might as well hang cheese around my neck."

Stallone: "You're not a rat. You're a witness. A witness bringing down the most dangerous players in New York— Porscha, Estaban Sanchez, the Gambinos. You're doing the country a favor."

Pete stared him down, eyes dead.

Big Pete: "Country don't mean shit when you're in the life. Loyalty does. Honor. Blood in, blood out. I've seen men get tortured for blinkin' wrong at the wrong boss. Now I'm spilling everything for a sandwich and a Kevlar vest."

He took a long pull from his cigar, silence hanging heavy.

43

Stallone: "Let's talk Porscha. You say she's the point of contact?"

Big Pete: "She is the operation. That girl ain't just movin' bricks—she's runnin' Sanchez's entire East Coast pipeline. Medellín's finest, straight into the ports in Newark, Jersey, Brooklyn. She's flooding the streets with coke—clean shipments, cartel-insulated. Every ounce's protected by badge money, judges on the take, and half the fuckin' city council."

Stallone: "And the Mafia?"

Big Pete: "She's got 'em by the balls. Gambinos, Luccheses, even a few old-timers from Chicago. She provides the weight and they push it through the street crews. She doesn't sell like a dealer—she distributes like a general. Ten keys at a time. Hundred bricks a month. Every family gets their cut. And if they don't play ball? She sends someone who makes sure they never play again."

He shook his head slowly.

Big Pete: "She took out Vince Calabrese on his daughter's wedding day. That's sacrilege, Stallone. That's the fuckin' Bible in the underworld. She had shooters dressed like waiters. Fifteen dead. Blood all over the wedding cake. That's who you're dealin' with."

Stallone: "She's not untouchable."

Big Pete: "You better hope she is. 'Cause if she finds out who's talkin'? I won't just be dead. I'll be erased."

The fire cracked in the silence. Stallone didn't respond. He just scribbled something on his clipboard and left Pete to the ghosts in his cigar smoke.

***

The matte black 2019 Mercedes-Benz G63 AMG purred low like a beast at rest, parked beneath a flickering streetlamp just outside Morningside Park, directly across from the Manhattan police station. It was just after 11:17

p.m., the night soaked in silence but for the occasional siren wailing in the distance and the static hum of neon buzzing against glass windows nearby.

In the backseat, Porscha sat poised—legs crossed, diamond-cut nails tapping against the cold leather armrest. Dressed in a black Valentino trench, crocodile skin Louboutins, and a blood-red silk blouse unbuttoned just enough to show a sliver of her tattooed collarbone, she radiated authority. Her iced-out choker sparkled like a snake waiting to strike. Beneath the luxury, she was a blade wrapped in velvet—silent, sharp, and ready.

Beside her, Rakim, her second-in-command, leaned forward slightly, eyes scanning the park through the tinted window. His Glock sat between his thighs, half-exposed under his peacoat.

"That's him," Rakim muttered, spotting the jittery silhouette pacing nervously near the broken park bench. "Five minutes late. You want me to handle it?"

Porscha didn't answer. She simply blinked slowly, her lashes casting long shadows across her cheekbones. Then she opened the door herself.

The thud of her Louboutins stepping onto wet pavement echoed louder than the wind.

The informant, a wiry man named Cree, turned toward the sound and froze. He looked confused—he thought he was only talking to Rakim. But then the door shut, and Porscha came toward him like midnight in motion.

Even in the dim park light, her presence was unmistakable. Her face was sculpted like a statue from wrathful marble—flawless, but cold. Her lips were painted the same deep crimson as the silk beneath her coat. The diamond pistol grip tucked under her jacket peeked out just enough to remind him: This wasn't just a conversation.

"You Cree?" she asked.

He nodded, with his voice stuck somewhere between fear and disbelief. "Y-yeah. I—I thought…"

"You thought wrong."

Her heels crushed a patch of wet gravel as she stepped closer. She didn't blink. Didn't smile. Didn't extend a hand. Only waited. Let the tension drown him.

Cree cleared his throat, eyes darting back toward the precinct. No one looked. No one saw.

He swallowed hard. "I ain't here to cause trouble. I just... look, a few nights ago, I was at this pool hall out in Yonkers. Nothing fancy. Real greasy spot. And these two guys— Pauly's men, I know them from way back—they didn't even recognize me. I was three stools down."

She didn't interrupt. Just stared. A slow rage started flickering behind her gaze.

Cree rubbed his hands together, trying to stay calm. "They were drunk, loud, real loose with they mouths. Talkin' like they was untouchable. One of them, the short one with the glass eye, kept braggin' about 'how that nigga Lance ain't see it comin'. Said they aired the whole car out. Said it was a message."

Porscha's eyes didn't blink. Her breathing slowed.

"They was laughin', sayin' how they emptied P90s into the ride, called it a 'car wash.' Kept repeatin' how 'that bitch Porscha gon' learn not to front on Pauly.'"

Cree hesitated.

Porscha leaned in an inch, her voice low. "Say that last part again."

His voice trembled. "They said... you needed to be reminded who runs shit. That Lance was a warning. One of them said, 'She pretty, but she not bulletproof.'"

Silence hung between them. Porscha's jaw clenched. Her eyes, those predator's eyes, never left his. Her face didn't move, but a vein near her temple pulsed.

Rakim stepped out of the G-Wagon now, leaning against the hood but staying back.

Cree kept talking. "They even named the shooter. Said some young dude from Red Hook—Juggz—was the one who actually pulled the trigger. They gave him fifty bands and a brick just to make the shot. Said Pauly wanted it fast, messy, and final."

Porscha finally blinked, just once, slowly. Her voice was a whisper. "You heard all this sitting three stools down?"

"I swear. I didn't say nothin'. Just sipped my drink and kept my head down. But I know what I heard. Word for word."

She pulled a small black envelope from her coat, thick with cash—a hundred thousand in fresh bands—and held it out.

"You work for me now."

Cree's eyes widened. "For real?"

"I don't repeat myself."

He grabbed the envelope like it might vanish. She stepped closer, nose almost touching his.

"If you lie to me..." she whispered, her tone turning venomous, "I won't send shooters. I'll come myself. And you'll wish it was a car wash."

Her voice lingered in his ears like poison.

Then she turned and walked back to the G-Wagon—hips swaying like a queen, expression unreadable, except for the glint of murder rising behind her lashes.

The doors shut. The engine growled to life.

Inside the G-Wagon, Rakim glanced at her.

"Boss?"

Porscha stared forward, silent.

Then, in a voice colder than steel: "Rivers of blood is about to flow that I promise you."

Chapter 7

The stale scent of burnt coffee lingered in the precinct's breakroom. The overhead light buzzed faintly, casting long shadows across the wall. Detective Flowers leaned back in his chair, sleeves rolled to his elbows, eyes bloodshot from too many nights without sleep.

Detective Boatwright stood by the window, arms crossed, staring out at the quiet city. But neither of them felt peace. Not tonight

"You know what this is, right?" Boatwright muttered

Flowers nodded slowly. "Yeah. It's a goddamn war. We got shootouts in front of nightclubs, high-level bodies dropping, witnesses disappearing. And the ones still breathing? Too scared to talk."

"Lance getting lit up outside Mercedes like that…" Boatwright shook his head. "Over three hundred rounds. That wasn't just a hit—that was a declaration."

Flowers sighed. "And not long before that, Cedric Harper's wife and brother get executed in their own brownstone. No signs of forced entry. Clean. Professional."

"Now we're hearing whispers. Gambino names. Cartel connections. The feds don't want to touch it. Crouton's rattled. You feel it too, right?"

"Yeah." Flowers rubbed his temples. "This ain't just about drugs or turf. This is power. Politics. Money so old it don't got no face."

Boatwright turned from the window. "You know who's making the calls?"

Flowers hesitated. "I got my guesses. Mayor Rapkim keeps popping up in the background. So does Attorney Salini. They're not holding guns, but they're handing out shields. And then there's Trayvon—used to be under the radar, now he's flying private jets with cartel lawyers."

Boatwright's jaw tightened. "And Porscha. She's not just some grieving club owner. She's moving like a boss. Like she's been trained by killers."

Flowers leaned in. "These ain't random killings. These are chess moves. And we're playing checkers."

"Then we better learn fast," Boatwright said. "Because someone's cleaning house. And we might be next on the list."

The highway stretched silent under a velvet black sky, flanked by thick, unbending woods. No traffic. No witnesses. Just shadows, still trees, and the cold flicker of moonlight slicing through the canopy like a warning whispered in silver.

In the back of a sleek, armored 2023 Cadillac Escalade, Sammy "The Don" Castellani, a fossil from the golden age of mob power, scrolled through his phone. He looked out of place in the glow of the dome light—silver hair slicked back, face carved by decades of blood and respect. Time hadn't touched him so much as learned to walk around him.

The road curved ahead. Then—trouble.

An SUV sat dead in the middle of the lane, hazard lights pulsing like a heartbeat. A crumpled deer lay across the pavement, its body twisted. A lone woman stood beside it, her silhouette tense, backlit by her high beams.

In the front seat, the driver squinted. "Looks like she hit a deer," he muttered

Sammy barely glanced up.

"Jesus Christ. Just go around her.

The Escalade slowed to a crawl. The woman paced, her movements erratic—hands trembling, eyes locked on the

49

deer like she couldn't believe it was dead. A civilian, by all appearances. Harmless. Fragile.

The window rolled down with a hum.

"You alright, miss? You're blocking the whole—"

She turned.

And that's when the world split open.

From the trees, two men in black hoodies exploded into motion—AR-15s already mid-scream. The night lit up with muzzle flashes. Glass shattered like a storm of crystal. Bullets tore through the windshield and the driver's chest with no mercy. Blood misted the air.

Sammy's voice roared from the back. "What the fuck?"

Too late.

The passenger door was yanked open like paper. The woman moved with calm, unbothered elegance. In her hand, a sleek pistol with a silencer already screwed on tight.

She walked to the back door.

No words. No warning.

Four tight shots.

His skull cracked open like a promise broken. Blood spattered across cream leather. Fragments of bone and power hit the windows as Sammy slumped, no longer a Don—just dead meat in an expensive suit.

She paused, breathing once—slow and deliberate. Her heels clicked against the asphalt as she leaned in close, eyes locked on his ruined face.

"Message sent," she whispered.

Then, a final round to the temple—clean, efficient. She smiled as she pulled the trigger.

Behind her, the two shooters sprinted. One dove into her SUV, the other peeled off in a black Charger waiting just off-road.

Tires squealed. Engines howled.

Then—nothing.

The Escalade sat idling, bathed in silence. Sinatra's "Fly Me to the Moon" floated softly through the blood-splattered speakers. Red pooled beneath the door. And the night swallowed everything whole.

***

Porscha lounged in a black leather armchair, one leg crossed over the other, a slow-burning cigar smoldering between her fingers. The flickering screen before her showed the aftermath—NYPD cruisers crawling over the scene, detectives ducking under yellow tape, news anchors fumbling to explain the carnage.

She watched without blinking.

"Let the rats wonder who lit the fire," she said, exhaling smoke in a ribbon.

Behind her, Rakim stood with his arms folded, his presence heavy but quiet.

"Sammy wasn't even in this war," he said.

Porscha didn't look away from the screen.

"Exactly."

Her lips curled into something between satisfaction and warning.

"Now they'll all wonder... if they all are involved."

***

The sharp scent of mahogany, leather, and imported smoke lingered in the air. A flat screen mounted to the office wall murmured in the background, casting its glow across polished wood and silent tension.

"Sammy Castellani, longtime mob figure, was gunned down tonight in what NYPD is calling a targeted execution..."

Footage rolled across the screen, a shot-up black Escalade riddled with bullets like a battlefield relic. Blood soaked the pavement. Police lights danced in chaos while yellow tape flapped in the wind like a warning flag to the underworld.

Lucchese sat frozen behind his desk. Draped in a double-breasted navy suit, he looked every bit the refined killer his reputation promised. His eyes were locked on the screen, expression unreadable—but rage simmered beneath his stillness. Each bullet hole replayed in slow motion, like open wounds burned into memory.

The door creaked.

Little John stepped inside without a word. His sweats sagged low, a diamond chain swinging across his chest, and his fitted cap was turned backward. He lowered his head respectfully before taking the seat across from the Don.

Lucchese didn't glance at him. He flicked his silver lighter open with precision, lit the cigar handed to him, and took a long, measured drag. Smoke curled from the corner of his lips, lazy and deliberate.

His voice was low and even. "Who the fuck would sign their name… on a death certificate like that?"

Little John shifted in his seat.

"I don't know," he said. "But two weeks ago? Porscha's club got lit up. One of her top men—Lance—got aired out like a dog in the street."

Lucchese turned to him then, slow and cold.

"And now," Little John continued, "less than seventy-two hours later, Sammy the Don gets turned into Swiss cheese on a back road—with military-grade heat? What are the odds, Don Lucchese? What are the fuckin' odds?"

Lucchese leaned back—not dismissively, but as if settling into calculation.

"I don't believe in odds," he said. "I believe in patterns. And this pattern stinks of something deliberate."

He reached for the remote, turned off the television, and let silence fill the room like smoke.

"Sammy wasn't just anybody," he said. "He sat at this table for twenty-five years. Took a bullet in '98 for the Commission. He was old school. His murder is an insult to the entire Five."

Little John nodded.

"Now everybody's jumpy," he said. "Colombians calling my burner, asking if we're going to war. Gambino's want to retaliate—but nobody knows who to shoot. Half of 'em think it was Porscha. The other half blame Escobar."

Lucchese narrowed his eyes. "Porscha ain't stupid. She's dangerous but calculated. If she did this, she wanted us to know she could. But I'm not convinced."

He flicked ash into the tray and let the silence stretch.

"Somebody's throwing rocks," he muttered, "and hiding their fucking hands."

He stood then, walking toward the floor-to-ceiling window that overlooked the city. The lights of Brooklyn, Queens, and beyond glittered in the distance—his empire illuminated and exposed.

"I want a sit-down," he said. "Not just Gambino. Not just Colombo. All Five Families. Staten Island, Queens, Manhattan, The Bronx, Brooklyn. Bring in the Latin Kings rep. The Dominicans. Even that quiet Russian in the uptown apartment. If someone's breaking the code... we break them."

Little John raised an eyebrow. "If it's Porscha?"

Lucchese turned, his stare ice cold.

"Then we bury her. Clean. Loud enough for the world to hear it. Quiet enough that no one sees it coming."

He returned to his desk and rested both hands on the wood, knuckles tight.

"But if it's someone else," he growled, "if someone's trying to pit us against each other... start a war from the inside..."

The words faded for a beat. Then his voice dropped lower.

"I'll rain bodies on this city until the East River turns red. I'll burn every ounce of product. Shut down ports. Strip rackets bare. Make everyone bleed—until whoever's behind this begs me for a bullet."

Little John swallowed. "You want me to start making calls?"

"No," Lucchese said. "I want you to show up at every door. In person. No phones. No wires. We do this old school."

He pressed the cigar into the ashtray, crushing the ember flat.

"And when we sit down," he said, eyes locked, voice like a promise from Hell, "anyone who lies… will fucking die."

***

Red and blue lights pulsed through the trees, slicing the night into jagged pieces. Police tape stretched from a low-hanging branch to the bent bumper of the Escalade, cutting the woods in half like a yellow scar. Crime scene techs stepped carefully around the shell casings that dotted the damp earth like scattered seeds—dozens of them. Numbered markers blinked against the grass, catching the glow of forensic lights.

Detective Simone Flowers stood at the edge of it all, hands buried in the pockets of her trench coat, her jaw tight, lips pressed flat. Her eyes didn't blink. They tracked the carnage with methodical calm—taking in the glass, the blood, the bullet holes that clustered like tumors across the windshield.

Her partner, Detective Alan Boatwright, was crouched low by the driver's side door. The Escalade's once-gleaming black finish was now a canvas of violence—splattered red, punctured, shredded. He hovered a gloved hand near the bullet pattern without touching it.

"Jesus Christ," he muttered. "This wasn't a hit. This was an execution."

Flowers stepped forward, boots brushing against a spent casing. "Sprayed from both sides," she said. "Precision work. They boxed the vehicle in—driver had no choice but to stop. Look at the angles. Two ARs minimum, crossfire pattern. Somebody walked up for the final shot."

She pointed to the shattered windshield, where a clean burst had gone straight through the glass.

"That wasn't panic. That was practiced."

Boatwright rose slowly, brushing his gloves together as if trying to shake off the weight of what he'd just seen.

"Sammy Castellani," he said, almost to himself. "Old-school capo. Back in the eighties, guy was tossing bodies in the East River like he was skipping stones."

"Madman," Flowers replied. "But connected. You don't just touch Sammy without stirring the whole Five. Whoever did this? They didn't just start a war… they signed their name in blood."

He circled around to the passenger side, eyes narrowing. The rear window was a spiderweb of fractured glass. Beyond it, the interior told the rest of the story—blood mist, skull fragments, the pink-gray smear of brain matter across the headrest. Entry wounds. Clean headshots.

"He never stood a chance," he said quietly.

Boatwright exhaled. "Porscha's club got hit last week. One of her top guys—Lance—got lit up. You thinking what I'm thinking?"

"If she didn't pull the trigger," Flowers said, "she damn sure pulled the strings."

The wind moved through the trees in a low whistle, rustling the crime scene tape. Somewhere deeper in the borough, sirens echoed faintly, hollow and distant.

Boatwright stared at the bullet-ridden SUV. "But why Sammy? He wasn't in play."

"Exactly," Flowers said. "He was clean. That's why it's a message."

Boatwright's eyes narrowed. "A loud one."

Flowers nodded once. Her voice was cold, final.

"Someone's playing a dangerous game, Boat. The kind where bodies don't just drop… they disappear."

They looked at each other—no more words between them, just the weight of something massive beginning to shift.

Boatwright spoke softly, almost hesitant.

"You think this ends at Sammy?"

"No," Flowers said, already turning back toward the forest of red and blue lights.

"Sammy was the start."

Chapter 8

The air down at the Brooklyn docks was thick with salt, diesel, and quiet menace. Massive steel containers groaned as they were lowered from the freighter, each one a silent testament to how deep the game really ran. Under flickering floodlights, Porscha stood back, watching her crew in motion—sharp, silent, and dressed in tactical black.

They moved like shadows, cutting seals, inspecting crates, giving tight nods. This was no routine drop. What Escobar Sanchez had sent was ten times the expected shipment—pure, untouched cocaine stacked floor to ceiling in all ten containers. It wasn't a gift. It was pressure. A challenge.

Porscha didn't blink. But her jaw clenched behind her nude gloss lips.

She stood tall in the shadows wearing black stilettos, fitted jeans, a cropped designer jacket and beneath it, her chrome-plated Desert Eagle. Her long jet-black hair was pulled back in a sleek ponytail. Even at night, in the grit and fog of the port, she looked untouchable. Deadly.

She pulled out her phone and dialed her father.

It rang twice before Trayvon picked up.

"Yeah, baby girl," he said, his voice low, gravel thick.

"This ain't what we agreed on," Porscha said, eyes scanning the bustling dock. "It's ten times more. You know that, right?"

"I know. Escobar said it's the last one for a while. He wants you to stretch it."

Porscha's eyes narrowed. Her crew had started loading the crates into blacked-out box trucks. They knew the drill—burner plates, wiped GPS, no paper trail.

"You were supposed to be here."

"I had to tie up some loose ends," Trayvon answered.

Porscha sucked her teeth. "Again?"

There was silence on the line.

"I'm upstate," he finally said. "Hudson River."

Her brows arched. "What are you doing all the way up there?"

"You remember Judge Smith?"

Porscha exhaled through her nose. "Of course, I remember him. He wanted to play hardball when we was trying get Sanchez son out of jail. We had to kidnap his whole damn family. I remember that son of a bitch."

"What about him?" she asked.

"He's been sleeping in the river six months now. Wrapped in bricks and guilt. Tonight, I'm waking him up."

Trayvon stood at the edge of a crumbling riverbank, moonlight casting cold silver across the surface of the Hudson. A small boat floated nearby, anchored by a body wrapped in layers of plastic and rusted chains—chains Trayvon had carefully broken tonight. Time had bloated the corpse of Judge Smith, but the face beneath the plastic was still recognizable. Moss clung to the wrapping like decay come alive.

If anyone found him now, the whole system would bleed.

Trayvon lit a cigar, the flame briefly illuminating his face. Calm. Calculated. Dangerous.

"If I want to move a few pieces off the board," he murmured into the phone, "old bones gotta rise. Let the cops find him. Let panic set in."

Back at the docks, Porscha paced, watching her last two trucks pull off with the product. She slowed her breath, but her eyes stayed sharp, cold.

"You're starting a war."

"No," Trayvon said. "I'm just exposing one that never ended."

"You should've been here with me," she said softly.

"Make sure everything gets to the warehouse. I'll be back before sunrise."

"I love you."

"I love you too."

The call ended.

The sea breeze hit her sharp. Porscha turned toward the last container as one of her crew approached.

"All ten secured, boss. No trackers. Warehouse sweep is clean."

She gave a single nod.

"What now?"

Porscha stared toward the water, her voice low, flat, lethal. "Now we show Escobar we don't panic. We don't fold."

Her stilettos echoed against the concrete as she turned toward her bulletproof SUV. The night wasn't quiet anymore. Not really. It was filled with moves behind moves.

"And if anybody ever thinks about crossing me again..." she added, "they'll end up like that judge—rotting in silence until I decide they scream. Found the body..."

***

The basement of the winery sat beneath the earth like a tomb—cool, silent, soaked in the weight of history and heat. Old barrels lined the walls like sleeping soldiers, and the air was thick with the scent of wine, stone, and war. A single bulb buzzed above the long oak table, casting shadows over the hard faces gathered there. Everyone knew why they were summoned. No one moved. No one dared speak first.

Porscha stepped through the heavy door like judgment itself. All black. Leather coat trailing behind her, boots cold and deliberate on the stone floor. A silence rippled across the room as she walked toward the head of the table, her eyes slicing through each man like a scalpel. No smiles. No nods. Just presence.

She didn't sit.

"You remember what the fuck we did two years ago?"

Her voice was calm—but lined with razor wire.

"We stood on business. We didn't flinch. Didn't fold. They said we couldn't go up against the mafia. That we'd burn out fast, fall apart like every other hungry crew before us."

A pause.

"But we didn't. We stood tall. We bled. We buried men. And then we made them kneel."

Porscha's gaze locked on Rakim—her enforcer. Then to Paris—her cold-blooded strategist. Then Corn—her silent killer. All of them stone-faced, waiting.

"We lost Lance. And that shit still stings. He was family. He died but when we was at war, he put bullets into those bastards who thought we were playing checkers, while they moved in with chess. But guess what?"

She leaned in. Her voice turned steel.

"They didn't win. We took Manhattan. Not with votes. Not with press. With blood, murder, and extortion. We carved out turf with gunfire and dragged old kings off their thrones. We showed the mafia—and the world—that we ain't just in this. We own this."

She finally sat—slow and deliberate. The silence in the room felt like it was holding its breath.

"This life? Ain't for the weak. Every time we leave the house, we might not come back. That's what makes it real. That's what makes it ours."

She flicked her silver lighter. Flame sparked. She lit a cigarette and took a long, slow drag, the smoke curling around her like a ghost.

"And now we're going to war. With everybody. The Luccheses are already bleeding. Escobar's trying to regroup.

The Irish crews want back in. The Russians think we tired. We're not."

She stood again.

"From this point on, we don't play defense. We press. Every angle. Every borough. Every rival crew, every whisper of opposition—they get crushed. Period."

She pointed.

"Rakim—you get me everything on the docks. Crate numbers, names, shipments. If it ain't ours, it's a target. No hesitation."

"Paris—I need Harlem locked down. Top to bottom. From the diners to the trap houses. I want ears in every barbershop, bodega, and betting joint."

"Corn—my eyes and my blade. I want snipers in place across Manhattan. Rooftops, alleys, penthouses. Quiet pressure. If they move, we strike."

She placed both palms on the table, her stare burning into them.

"We're not scared of nobody. Not the mafia. Not the feds. Not the ghosts of the past. We are the new era. The fear. The dark undercurrent they hoped would fade."

The room stayed frozen. Every man locked in.

"We lost Lance, yeah. But we don't lose momentum. This war we're stepping into? It's for him. It's for all of us. For the legacy."

Thunder rumbled faintly in the distance.

Porscha whispered, lips barely moving, eyes burning.

"Let 'em come. Let 'em try. This ain't a warning. It's a funeral notice."

She took one last drag and crushed the cigarette into the table's ashtray.

"And I want blood in the wine by sunrise."

Chapter 9

The lights inside the 17th Precinct's basement briefing room were low, harsh, buzzing with tension. The city's power players in law enforcement sat at a long steel table—paperwork scattered, photos clipped to corkboards, red string running between names and crime scenes on a tactical map of New York Cit

Detective Flowers leaned forward in her chair, stone-faced, blazer unbuttoned, service weapon holstered at her hip. Beside her sat Detective Boatwright—younger, more erratic, tapping a pen against his notebook but saying nothing. Across from them, Captain Lawson stood with his arms crossed, a man whose patience had been scraped thin by too many funerals and too little justice.

At the head of the room, in front of the digital board, stood FBI Senior Chief Henry Goldwyn—graying, stiff, but still commanding—and FBI Special Agent Sampaio, silent but coiled with energy like a loaded spring

Goldwyn cleared his throat, tossed a manila file onto the table, and broke the silence.

"Two years ago, the crime rate in New York hit a level we hadn't seen since the eighties. Bodies were dropping like flies. The streets were soaked in cocaine, blood, and fear. The Mafia was getting hit. The cartel was responding. It was open warfare—and we were caught in the middle."

He hit a button on the remote. The board behind him lit up with gruesome crime scene photos, docks lit with muzzle flashes, cars shredded with bullets, restaurant floors soaked in crimson. "That was wave one. And now wave two... is here. It's already started."

No one said a word. Sampaio finally stepped forward, jaw clenched.

"The Wedding Massacre—Sunday, the 15th. Mob boss Mannino, his daughter, his son-in-law, and eleven others executed at point-blank range in broad daylight at a private estate. The shooter team was professional. Surgical. Porscha sent the order. Personal retaliation—Mannino tried to have her killed."

He clicked the next slide, surveillance photos, license plates, schematics of the estate.

"That hit wasn't just revenge. It was a message. Porscha isn't hiding in shadows anymore. She's making her moves in public. And she's not just controlling a crew—she's running an empire."

Flowers crossed his arms.

"You think we don't know that? You think we haven't seen the bodies stacking up? Two of our own agents are dead. Confidential informant Joey was tortured and dumped in the Hudson. Jessica Vasquez—our embedded contact—got blown up with her own car four blocks from this precinct."

"This isn't a gang war," Captain Lawson snapped. "It's insurgency."

Sampaio's voice cut through the room like a blade. "No. It's worse than insurgency. It's organization. Porscha has structure. She's got military precision. Her people don't make mistakes. They disappear into the cracks. And when they hit, it's with purpose."

He pulled out another file—Porscha's inner circle.

"Rakim. Ex-enforcer. Gun charges buried in court. Walked clean. Paris—genius-level strategist, holds three fake passports, never photographed twice in the same city. Corny—silent killer, no prints, no trace. The only confirmed sighting was two years ago, leaving the scene of the

Mannino massacre. Lance? Dead. Buried with honors on their side like he was a martyr.

Goldwyn took back the floor. "Let's call this what it is. Porscha has declared war on the city of New York. And if we don't shut her down, we're looking at a collapse of everything—federal control, city order, judicial reach. She's already compromised judges, DAs, and half the street-level narcotics division."

Boatwright slammed his pen down.

"So what do we do? RICO? Wiretaps? Raids? She's got eyes everywhere. We make one move and they're gone before we hit the street."

"Then we stop thinking like cops," Flowers said quietly. "We start thinking like them."

The room stilled.

"You want to bring her down?" she continued. "Then we infiltrate. We burn her network from the inside. We flip her lieutenants. We hit the money. Follow the laundering trails. Shake the foundations. And when she's isolated? Then we move."

Goldwyn nodded.

"Agreed. But we can't hesitate. This city is a tinderbox. One more public hit—one more mass casualty event—and the mayor's office will pull funding, declare martial law, or worse. We'll lose the streets entirely."

Sampaio exhaled, slow and sharp.

"This isn't about cleaning up the city anymore. This is about stopping the woman who already owns it. And if we don't stop Porscha…"

He looked around the room. "There won't be a city left to save."

Chapter 10

The black Mercedes-Benz G63 crawled to a slow stop in front of Club Mercedes, its sleek frame reflecting the neon haze bleeding off the building's signage. The engine purred low, like a predator waiting to strike. The driver stepped out and opened the door.

Porscha emerged.

Hair laid, face carved like vengeance, heels clicking with intent. She didn't look around—she never had to. Everyone else looked at her. She walked into the club like it belonged to her. Because it did.

Inside, the girls froze when they saw her. Conversations died mid-sentence. Cell phones slid out of sight. Some shifted uncomfortably on stilettos they'd been standing in too long. Porscha scanned the floor with cold precision, her eyes sweeping across every dancer, hostess, bottle girl, and bartender. No one moved.

Without a word, she turned and headed upstairs.

At the top level, Paris—head of operations—stood inside her office, peering out the window. She watched as Porscha's security took position outside her door, blocking access like steel statues. Paris didn't need to be told—they were under orders.

Inside, Porscha sat like a queen returned to her throne. Paris entered moments later, her voice cautious.

"I didn't know you were coming by."

Porscha didn't smile. "That's a good thing."

Paris straightened up. "The money's coming along good. The girls are—"

"Good," Porscha cut her off. "Then let me see the numbers."

Paris hesitated for half a breath before grabbing the ledger from her desk. She handed it over. Porscha flipped through it slowly, the tension rising with every page turn.

Then she stopped.

Ruby.

Short. Again. Two weeks in a row.

Paris swallowed hard. She already knew what was coming. The last girl who came up short ended up rolled in industrial plastic and dumped behind a greasy burger joint on 87th. Her blood was still a rumor whispered behind locked dressing room doors.

Porscha closed the book.

"Go get her."

Paris didn't move.

Porscha's voice sharpened like a blade.

"Bitch, I said go get her. And bring her raggedy ass to me. Matter of fact—bring all the motherfucking girls."

Paris moved, legs shaky, but she knew better than to argue. Minutes later, the girls filed in. Silence thickened the air. Ruby tried to blend in, but Porscha's eyes found her instantly.

She stood. Walked straight up to her.

"Hand," Porscha demanded.

Ruby raised it, trembling.

Porscha reached into her coat and pulled out a razor. Silver. Clean. Sharp.

She pressed it into Ruby's open palm. Held her eyes the entire time.

"If you ever come up short on my money again," she whispered, voice like smoke and death, "I'll make this personal. I like you, Ruby… but I'll make you swallow this."

Ruby's knees buckled, but she didn't fall.

Porscha turned, addressing the entire room.

"This ain't no game. This ain't a maybe. If any one of you ever thinks for one second that I'm bluffing, remember the girl who bled out behind Burger Town. I will make an example. I will ruin your last breath. play with me if you want to.

Not a soul spoke.

Porscha stepped back, satisfied with the fear now thick in the room. She handed the razor back to Ruby and smiled—cold, cruel, and beautiful.

"Now get back to work now."

***

The steel door groaned as it swung open.

Detective Flowers stepped inside first, trench coat still damp from the night rain. Behind her, Agent Sampaio from the FBI followed, flanked by Officer Delgado. Their boots echoed across the tile, hard and deliberate. They didn't say a word at first—they just stared at the man in the corner.

Big Pete.

He sat low in the metal chair, one leg stretched out, cigar resting between his thick fingers, smoke curling to the ceiling. The overhead light made the sweat on his temple glisten like oil. His eyes followed them with the quiet of a man who had seen too much and lived through worse.

They stopped a few feet from the table.

Flowers finally broke the silence. "What do you know about Porscha that we don't?"

Agent Sampaio dropped a folder in front of him. "Your paperwork's through. Witness protection. New name. New address. New ghost to become."

Pete chuckled. It wasn't joy, it was nerves and nightmares wrapped in a laugh.

"You think that paper's gonna save me? You really don't know her."

Delgado leaned forward. "Then help us understand."

Big Pete took a slow pull from the cigar. "She came in like a wrecking ball. No finesse, no whispers. Just smoke, blood, and power. She didn't climb the ladder—she ripped it down and made her own. Porscha didn't ask for permission. She took what she wanted."

He flicked ash into the tray.

"People weren't just dying. They were vanishing. No trace. No warning. Porscha made it clear—this wasn't business. This was domination. She wanted every room to fall silent when her name came up. She made sure of it."

They watched as Pete's demeanor changed, voice tighter now.

"She started with Roberto. Tried to sit down, tried to play it cool. He brushed her off like she was just another loud pretty face. Two days later, he was shot down on Main Street, a bullet in his forehead because of the words his tongue spoke to her. He called her father a pig."

No one in the room flinched.

"She wasn't sending messages—she was writing scripture in blood."

He looked up, voice lowering.

"I know y'all think you got a handle on her but let me tell you something—if you don't hear from Frankie in the next two weeks, he's dead. And if he's dead, Porscha killed him. No doubt in my mind."

Flowers arched a brow. "Frankie tried to have her hit, didn't he?"

Pete nodded, eyes distant. "Tried. Failed. Porscha don't let shit go. You could come to her with God himself, and she'd still make you pay."

He leaned closer, eyes burning now.

"Y'all remember Sunday the 15th? The Wedding Massacre? Sixteen people dead including the groom, the preacher, and the saxophone player? That wasn't cartel spillover. That was Porscha! Porscha didn't just shoot the mob boss Mannino—she torched the venue to get her point across. She not scared of war."

He paused. Voice grim.

"Porscha... she puts fear in the devil's heart."

Delgado shifted his weight. The room felt colder.

"You wanna know how bad she is?" Pete whispered. "She's buried bodies so deep in the ground, the devil pays her rent now."

No one spoke.

Sampaio stepped back. Flowers just stared at Pete, like watching a man who already knew his tombstone's inscription.

Pete rubbed his face. "This woman ain't a criminal. She's not even human anymore. She's a force. A plague wearing heels and designer bags."

He stood slowly, dragging the last puff of his cigar before smashing it out.

"You don't hunt Porscha. You survive her. And if you ain't ready to watch your family disappear one by one—then you better walk away before your soul gets signed over, too."

He turned toward the one-way glass, then back at them.

"Before I say another word... I need a fucking drink."

They all looked at each other—and none of them said a thing.

Because deep down, they knew Pete wasn't warning them.

He was delivering their eulogies in advance.

Chapter 11

The bathroom light buzzed with a dying hum, casting a sickly yellow glow over the cracked mirror. Big Pete leaned forward, both hands pressed flat against the chipped porcelain sink, his broad shoulders rising and falling with ragged breaths. Sweat glistened on his bald head. His eyes—bloodshot, angry, broken—refused to blink. He couldn't look away from the man in the mirror.

A man he barely recognized anymore.

"You weak son of a bitch," he muttered, voice low and thick like gravel.

His fist struck the edge of the sink, hard. A crack spread through the porcelain like a spider web. Blood seeped from the split skin across his knuckles. He didn't flinch. Pain was welcome now. Pain meant he was still human, even if just barely.

"You were the monster in every fuckin' room," he hissed at his reflection. "You brought fear just by standin' there. Men shook when you smiled. And now look at you…"

He tilted his head, jaw trembling. "Now you're sittin' here talkin' to the feds—spillin' things you swore to die with."

The words tasted like rot in his mouth. Every confession, every whispered name, every detail handed over in cold rooms under fluorescent lights—it clawed at his soul. He'd never begged for his life before. Not until now. Not until the weight of all the bodies he helped bury started keeping him up at night.

"I bled for them. Killed for them. Families, mothers, kids… I said the word, and death followed. I was the fuckin' code."

He turned from the mirror and began to pace, the floor groaning beneath his boots. Memory after memory crashed through his mind—gun smoke, screams, flames, and silence. That long, cold silence after a job was done and a life was snuffed out.

And now? He was a ghost. A shadow in a safe house, hidden away by the very government he used to spit on.

"They trusted me," he said, more to himself than anything. "And I folded."

But something shifted in him. In the silence. In the blood on his hand. In the reflection he couldn't escape.

He stopped pacing.

His jaw clenched. A decision etched itself into his bones.

He walked over to the window and peered out. The street was still. Dim streetlamps barely lit the cracked pavement. No sirens. No voices. Just him—and the sound of everything he used to be, roaring in his chest.

"I can't live like this," he whispered. "Not like a fuckin' dog on a leash. Not beggin' for protection. I ain't built for this."

Pete moved fast after that. He slid on his coat, pulled his hoodie low, and tucked a knife that was in the kitchen drawer into the waistband of his jeans. He paused only once—right at the door—to glance back at the mirror. That man in there was dead.

He'd died the moment Pete opened his mouth to the feds.

"I'm gonna see Nick," he muttered. "He deserves to hear it from me."

Then he was gone.

He slipped out the back, quiet as smoke, every step practiced and precise. He knew the blind spots, knew when the agents posted up outside would be dozing or distracted. In less than a minute, Big Pete vanished into the shadows.

Not a trace. Not a whisper.
The rat was out of the cage.
And he was walking straight to the lion.

***

The steady crash of bowling balls echoed like distant thunder, layered over classic Motown humming through old speakers. Fluorescent lights flickered above the vintage lanes of Strike Gold Alley, a spot where nobody asked questions and everybody knew not to listen too closely.

Lucchese leaned back on the red leather booth, eyes narrowed behind his tinted glasses as he watched the old women bowl like it was Sunday mass. Matching league shirts, drinks sweating on the tables, purses clutched close. You'd never guess a war was simmering two feet behind them.

Nick "the Boss" sat beside him, silent, arms folded. No chains. No flash. Just steely eyes and a scarred knuckle tapping slowly against the laminated table. He looked like a man with a thousand ghosts and one more on the way.

Lucchese finally broke the silence. "Everybody's pointing fingers over Sammy the Don. Streets say cartel, feds whisper mafia, but it's too damn neat. Too surgical. He was old-school, but he didn't go out like one."

Nick didn't flinch. Just watched lane six as one of the ladies rolled a perfect strike.

"You think Porscha had a hand in it?" Lucchese asked carefully, eyes not leaving the lane. "She's been making moves. Big ones. Shaking trees we didn't even plant. What if she—"

Nick turned his head slowly, locking eyes. "Don't accuse her of anything.

Lucchese blinked. "I didn't—"

"You're doing that thing," Nick cut him off, voice low but sharp. "That fed-bait whisper shit. Last time someone so much as insinuated her hand in something, five families lost lieutenants, and Brooklyn ran red for six months."

Lucchese exhaled, nodding. "I get it. You trust her?"

Nick's jaw flexed. "I trust no one. But I respect power—and Porscha's power ain't built on gossip. It's concrete. It's blood. It's legacy."

He paused, watching a lady stumble as her ball veered into the gutter.

"She's carved out an empire, not a corner. But something is off. Sammy had secrets. Secrets that could burn whole bloodlines."

Lucchese leaned in. "Then what's the move?"

Nick stood, adjusting his jacket. Calm. Calculated. "I'll talk to her. Myself. Quiet. Direct. If she knows something, I'll know by the way she doesn't say it. But we don't move on Porscha unless we're ready to burn every bridge, church, and casket from here to Bogotá."

Lucchese gave a short nod. "Understood."

Nick looked down at the lanes. Another strike. Applause from the league ladies. He cracked a faint smile. "Funny, huh? Life's a lot like bowling. Set 'em up just to knock 'em down."

Lucchese chuckled. "Difference is, in our world, the pins bleed."

Nick stepped away from the booth, his shoes echoing across the alley's polished floor. War was always one conversation away—and tonight, he was about to have one with a queen who never bowed.

***

Sunday night, around 8:39 pm. The stars are out, but war clouds hang heavy in the air.

The sleek black SUV pulled up to the private marina under armed escort. Nick the Boss stepped out, flanked by three of his men—each one strapped, eyes cutting through the dark like searchlights. The water shimmered under moonlight, quiet and still, as if it knew what kind of conversation was about to happen.

Porscha's yacht sat like a floating palace at the end of the dock—elegant, powerful, dangerous. She greeted Nick at the gangway, her silk wrap flowing in the breeze, diamonds glittering at her wrist. She kissed him on the cheek, held his face a moment—respect, but not submission.

"Come aboard," she said with a half-smile. "We need to talk."

The men were escorted to the back while Nick and Porscha sat at the top deck, sipping on Yamazaki 55, the rarest Japanese whiskey in the world. She leaned back in her chair, crossing one leg over the other. The night wind played with her hair.

"What do you know about Sammy the Don?" Nick asked softly, watching her reaction.

She didn't blink. "Are you accusing me of something?"

"I'm asking," he said, sipping slow. "Because last time people assumed, we were cleaning blood off the streets for six months."

She nodded, respecting the memory. "Then don't assume. Just follow me."

They took the yacht for a slow cruise along the mountain ridge until it reached a secluded view of the Apple Mountain Resort. She handed him a pair of military-grade binoculars and pointed across the lake to the massive glass windows of the exclusive lounge.

"Look."

Nick adjusted the lens. Inside, he spotted Pauly, one of their own, drinking and laughing with a few of his crew.

"So?" Nick asked, still watching.

"Keep looking," Porscha said, her voice ice smooth. "To the right."

He panned to the side—and froze.

Cedric Harper, sharp suit, signature cigar, leaned against the marble bar. Pauly walked up to him casually, whispered something, and both men laughed like old devils sharing secrets.

Nick lowered the binoculars. His jaw tensed.

"Cedric Harper?" he muttered. "He's running for mayor."

Porscha's voice sharpened. "Yeah. And Pauly's been feeding him everything. Information, locations. I've been watching them for two months. I knew Pauly was behind the hit at Club Mercedes—when Lance was murdered in the parking lot, in the middle of sex. I knew he had my club shot up. I gave it time, hoping y'all would figure it out yourselves. What better way to start a campaign trail off than a war in the streets? Sammy the Don was murdered to start the war to make it look like it was me."

Nick stared down at the water, heavy silence between them.

She leaned in. "Now that you know, you got two weeks. Handle Pauly, or I will. Respectfully. But I'm not scared of war, Nick. Some lines you just don't cross. Killing my man? That was one."

Nick took one last look at Apple Mountain, then turned to her.

"That motherfucking pig," he whispered.

They clinked glasses. Not in celebration. But in agreement.

War wasn't coming. It was already here.

Chapter 12

Private bar lounge, deep in Brooklyn. Dim light. Red leather booths. Old-school jazz playing low. Whiskey breath and war in the air.

The back room was soundproof, thick walls soaked in secrets and blood. Four men sat in a tight circle. Nick the Boss, Lucchese, Frank Marino, and old man Gianni. Bottles of Johnnie Blue and Hennessy XO half-drunk, untouched cigars sitting on the table.

Nick leaned back, shoulders heavy. His jaw locked.

"She showed me everything," he said. "I saw it with my own fin' eyes. Pauly. Laughin'. Toastin' up with Cedric Harper like they childhood friends. You know that mother-f-er's runnin' for mayor?"

Lucchese's eyes twitched, his hand tightening around his glass.

"She gave me binoculars and a view from her yacht," Nick continued. "He was with Harper at Apple Mountain. Inside the glass lounge. Casual. Like he didn't have nothin' to hide. Like we some fucking' children."

Frank cursed under his breath. Gianni didn't move—stone still.

Lucchese said nothing. He was staring at the floor. Then he spoke, quiet but sharp.

"So Pauly killed Sammy. That's what you're tellin' me?"

Nick nodded once. "And Lance. Porscha's man. Top lieutenant. He was at Club Mercedes, in the parking lot, in the car—getting' some—when they hit him."

Lucchese's breath caught. "That was him? That hit was Pauly?"

"All of it. She's known for two months. She didn't move. She waited. Gave us the chance to do the right thing."

Lucchese stood up. Slowly. Poured his drink out on the rug like a funeral toast.

"She gave us two weeks, huh?" he said, voice low and hard. "Told you that straight?"

Nick looked up, frustrated. "Yeah. Two weeks. Or she's handling it herself. And I get it—but that ain't sit right with me. Like she's pressin' us. Like she's checkin' us on our own fuckin' turf."

Lucchese spun fast, slammed his fist into the wall, cracking wood. Bottles jumped.

"Because we fin' deserved it!" he barked. "We let that rat sit at the table. We let him whisper in our fin' ears, kiss our cheeks, while he lined up bodies behind our backs."

Frank stepped in. "Boss—"

"Shut up, Frank."

Lucchese looked at Nick, breathing heavy.

"She had every right to snap. She didn't. You know what kinda restraint that takes? They killed her man, Nick. Her fuckin' heart. And she still waited. She didn't start a war, didn't hit back. She showed more honor than we did."

Nick nodded slowly. "I hear you. I do. But it's still a line crossed. Two weeks is pressure. Ain't nobody ever gave me a deadline."

Lucchese stepped close, his eyes fire and ash.

"This ain't about pride, Nick. This is about respect. Pauly took out our Don. He hit us from inside. Porscha didn't do that. She gave us a gift—time. So, stop takin' it personal."

Nick dropped his head. "It's personal to me because it makes us look weak."

Lucchese leaned in. "You wanna look weak? Do nothin'. You wanna remind everybody who the fuck we are? Handle Pauly. Public. Brutal. Final."

Frank broke his silence. "What's the play?"

Lucchese stared into the shadows.

"We don't just kill him. We hurt him first. Mentally. Physically. We drag out every secret he ever whispered. Every dollar he stashed. Every lie he told. And then we erase him like he never fuckin' existed."

He looked around the room.

"Get ready. We got less than two weeks to make this look like justice, not revenge. 'Cause if Porscha moves first—if she draws blood before we do? We lose every inch of face we got left."

Nick stood, chin squared now.

"Then we start tonight."

Lucchese nodded. "Tonight."

Gianni raised his glass. "To the fall of rats."

They drank. No toasts. No smiles. Just silence, loaded glasses clinking together.

The war wasn't coming.

It had a name now.

Pauly.

And soon, it'd have a funeral.

***

The stink of rot clung to the woods like a curse. Somewhere beyond the yellow tape, the buzz of flies hummed over the carcass of justice—Judge Brad Smith, once untouchable, now barely recognizable beneath the decay.

Detective Flowers adjusted his belt and stepped out of the cruiser, slow and heavy-footed. His round belly moved with a rhythm of its own, but the man was sharp—don't let the frame fool you. He'd cracked more cases than most of the fresh-faced agents sniffing around the scene.

Chief Lawson stood waiting near the body, his jaw locked tight, arms folded like he was holding the trees back with sheer tension.

"You see the chain?" Lawson asked, voice dry.

Flowers grunted, then crouched beside the tarp as the coroner lifted it back with gloved hands. There it was. That thick gold chain—the one Judge Smith never took off. Even ten months underground couldn't hide it.

"Hell," Flowers muttered. "He's been missing that long. We all thought he ran."

Lawson nodded. "Turns out he didn't run. He got disappeared."

Flowers scanned the area. CSI was everywhere. K9 dogs sniffed through underbrush like they were chasing ghosts. The scent trail was cold, but it was clear—Brad was dumped, not buried. Whoever did this didn't care if he was found. Or maybe... they cared when.

"There's more to this," Flowers said, voice low. "Brad had his fingers in too many pies. Judges don't vanish without a ripple."

"Unless someone made the water still," Lawson said grimly.

From across the trees, a tech raised a hand. "We found fibers—looks like upholstery, high-end vehicle, maybe European."

Flowers stood up, grunting. "So, whoever dumped him rides smooth."

Lawson tapped his radio. "Where's Boatwright?"

"Out following a witness. Big case. Cartel-linked," came the reply.

Flowers side-eyed Lawson. "You think this ties into the Sanchez operation?"

Lawson's silence was telling. He didn't know—but he had a feeling. And feelings in this city had body counts.

Back at the edge of the scene, a fresh detective walked up holding a sealed bag. "We pulled this from the chain."

Inside was a small tag, engraved with initials—J.S. Clean, untouched. Like someone wanted them to know exactly who they were dealing with.

Lawson stared at it. "It's him."

Flowers turned toward the trees. "This is a message. Someone wanted Brad gone but not forgotten."

Lawson nodded. "Someone powerful."

Flowers looked back one more time at the body. He didn't say it out loud, but something twisted in his gut. The way the judge disappeared… the way no one ever found Frankie.

His instincts barked like a dog behind a fence. Something else was rotting. Something they hadn't found yet.

And they didn't even know the worst of it was still waiting in a small house across town—Jessica, lifeless, swinging by the neck, whispering the second half of a warning nobody had heard yet.

Chapter 13

The Bronx – 1:17 AM

The meat hooks swayed gently in the walk-in. A light hum from the cooler buzzed behind the walls. The air was sharp with steel, salt, and silence.

Lucchese sat alone under a low bulb in the back room. No guards. No noise. Just him, a pack of Camels, and a loaded truth that was about to be spoken.

The door creaked. Donnie stepped in, shut it behind him. Didn't need to be told to sit.

Lucchese lit a cigarette, took one drag, then exhaled slowly—like he was settlin' into a confession, but one lined with razor wire. "You were with me the night we buried Sammy, right?"

Donnie nodded. Barely.

"You remember what that felt like?"

"Yeah."

"Good. 'Cause what I'm about to say, it's stitched with that same kind of sorrow."

Lucchese leaned forward, elbows on the table, the cherry on his cigarette glowing in the dark.

"Pauly is the reason that man is dead."

He let the words sit. Heavy. Truth didn't need to shout when it cut that deep.

"He played both sides. Sat at our table, smiled in our faces, then ran his fin' mouth to the wrong people. Told 'em where Sammy would be. Leaked the route. That's why The

Don died like a f-in' civilian, in the back of a goddamn car on a back road, like his life didn't mean somethin'."

Lucchese's jaw flexed, eyes hard.

"You know what Sammy was to me, Donnie. He brought me in when I was nothin' but a punk kid, boostin' radios off parked cars. Taught me this life. Fed me. Buried people for me. And that rat Pauly fed him to the wolves for what— money? Favor?"

Lucchese flicked ash into a dish shaped like a pig's skull.

"So now Pauly's gonna feel what I feel. Every day. Quietly. Permanently."

He slid a photograph across the table. Pauly's nephew. Young. Greasy smile. Work gloves in his back pocket. Scrap yard dog.

"That's his sister's boy. His blood. His light."

Lucchese tapped the photo. "You're gonna make that light go out."

Donnie didn't blink. "You want it loud or soft?"

Lucchese shook his head once.

"No noise. No mess. I want you to cut him outta the fin' world like he never existed. No grave. Nobody. Not even a whisper. I want Pauly to choke on not knowin'. Every time he walks past that scrapyard, he's gonna wonder if his nephew's bones are buried under the fenders. He's gonna lose his mind one sleepless night at a time."

He lowered his voice. Deadly calm.

"You find a way to get the kid to meet you—somewhere neutral. Keep it friendly. Business casual. Then you take him off the board. Quiet. Final. I don't want nobody askin' questions."

Lucchese opened a drawer beneath the table and pulled out a slim envelope—thick with cash, light with consequence. "This ain't just vengeance. This is a lesson. This is the kind of justice that don't get written in court records. This is Cosa Nostra, Donnie."

He slid it across. "You do this right... you don't just carry my name—you carry the ghost of Sammy Castellani with you."

Donnie nodded once. Voice low, locked in.

"He'll vanish like smoke, boss. Won't even be ash."

Lucchese stood slowly, walked to the freezer door. His hand gripped the handle, but he paused, turned back one last time. "And Donnie... if you got even an ounce of mercy left in you—kill it before you see him. This ain't business. This is family."

He pulled the door open, letting cold white light spill in like a morgue's breath.

Donnie stood, pocketed the photo and envelope. No more words. Just purpose.

**

The rain had started just after sundown, a light drizzle that made the streets shimmer under the city lights. But the crowd in front of City Hall didn't budge. New Yorkers stood shoulder to shoulder, soaked and steaming with anticipation, their umbrellas open like silent witnesses to a revolution in the making.

Cedric Harper stood center stage, dressed in a tailored navy suit with a blood-red tie, his face lit by harsh floodlights. A single microphone waited before him. No notes. No teleprompter. Just fire in his chest and war in his eyes.

He leaned forward, gripping the edge of the podium.

"New York City... I've had enough. Haven't you?"

The crowd answered with a rolling cheer, fierce and unrelenting. He let it rise, let it boil.

"Every night we bury our children—not from foreign wars, but from bullets five blocks from home. Our streets are owned by ghosts in sneakers, by cartel runners, by mafia shadows who think they still run this city. They treat our grief like a business."

Some in the crowd clapped. Others froze, watching carefully as the weight of his words hit.

"And I'm not afraid to say their names. The cartels? They're not just in Colombia anymore—they're right here in Harlem, in The Bronx, in Queens. The mafia? They've traded suits for judges' robes and sit in backrooms, laundering blood money through banks you trust. And Porscha—yeah, that Porscha—some of y'all worship her like she's royalty. She ain't no queen. She's a killer. In heels. In lace. In red lipstick. And her day is coming."

The reporters froze. Flashes exploded like gunfire. Somewhere in the crowd, a cartel spotter dialed a number and walked off.

But Cedric didn't stop.

"Our judges? Bought and sold. Our district attorneys? Quiet because they're scared, or dirty because they're paid. The system was supposed to protect us—but it's just another gang with a badge."

He slapped the podium hard enough to make the mic jump.

"Not under me. Not one more damn day."

The roar was deafening. Flags waved. Fists pumped. Every camera in the city was locked on him.

"I will burn every ounce of corruption to ash. I will tear these street kings and courtroom cowards from their thrones. You want justice for the mothers burying babies? You want peace for the fathers doing time, while real killers walk free? You want to stop being afraid to walk outside?"

He pointed at them like he was calling them to arms.

"Then vote for me. Not next year. Not after another funeral. Now."

The crowd exploded. Some in tears. Some in rage. Some just listening. But all of them felt it.

***

Just two blocks away, tucked inside the backseat of a blacked-out SUV, Porscha watched the whole thing unfold on the screen mounted behind the driver's seat. Smoke curled up from the fat cigar resting between her fingers, filling the cabin with the scent of Cuban spice and quiet fury. Her legs were crossed, black leather clinging to every curve, her expression unreadable beneath thick lashes and sharper thoughts. Rain tapped the window like a warning.

She took one long drag, then slowly exhaled, eyes still locked on Cedric's face as he stood behind the podium.

"He said my name," she muttered. Not shocked. Not scared.

Amused.

Pissed.

The driver said nothing. He knew better.

She flicked ash into a glass tray and narrowed her eyes as Cedric's voice echoed through the car's speakers.

"He wanna be famous?" she whispered. "I'll make him a fuckin' headline."

Her phone buzzed.

1   New Message – TRAYVON

"He dies. Make it loud."

She didn't type back. Just tapped the screen off, inhaled deep, and stared out into the rain-soaked streets of the city she ruled without question.

Now? Now, it was personal.

***

The city below buzzed like static. From the 22nd floor of the Hudson Grand Hotel, Cedric Harper could see the whole skyline—glittering towers, traffic veins, the bones of New York he'd promised to rebuild. The suite was all velvet and chrome, polished with money that wasn't his. His campaign manager booked it. But it was his cousin, Pauly, who covered the cost. Family support.

Or so he thought.

The clock blinked 2:17 AM. Cedric was still dressed—shirt unbuttoned, tie loosened, speech notes scattered across the glass coffee table. He poured himself a drink, hand trembling just enough to spill a splash.

His phone rang.

Unknown number.

He hesitated. Then answered.

"Hello?"

Silence.

Then her voice.

Velvet and venom.

"You fucked up, Cedric."

His breath caught. "Porscha?"

"You said my name on stage like you had the right. Like it wouldn't cost you anything."

He looked around the room, sudden tension cutting through the air.

"This ain't politics anymore, baby," she said. "This is personal."

The line went dead.

He turned slowly toward the front door.

A knock.

Soft. Deliberate.

His feet were stone as he crossed the room and opened it.

Porscha stood there. All-black bodysuit. Long coat flowing. Eyes rimmed in shadow and fire. Behind her, two men stepped forward—Rakim and Cory—each built like muscle made flesh, each silent as death.

Cedric's heart sank.

"No," he whispered. "No, Porscha... come on... you don't have to do this."

She stepped inside, slow, unbothered. Her eyes scanned the luxury suite like it was already a crime scene.

"You wanted to be famous," she said, calm and low. "Remember that. You begged for people to hear you."

"I was tryin' to help the city," Cedric said, voice cracking. "I was trying to clean it up. Your name—your name slipped, that's all, I swear to God—"

"You swore to cameras," she cut in, stopping just a few feet from him. "Not God."

Rakim closed the door behind them.

Cedric dropped to his knees.

"Porscha, please," he begged. "We grew up in the same streets. Come on, don't do this. You can have the campaign money, I'll drop out—I'll leave town. Please…"

Her face didn't change. No flicker of doubt. No pity. Just a slow, tired blink.

"You think I didn't know who paid for this room?" she whispered.

His eyes widened. "Pauly?"

She nodded once.

"And he already paid again—for the cleanup."

Cedric sobbed now, snot mixing with tears. "Please don't kill me."

She leaned in, kissed his forehead gently, then whispered in his ear. "You already dead. You just haven't hit the ground yet.

Then she stepped back.

Rakim and Cory grabbed him by the arms, dragged him screaming across the penthouse suite toward the floor-to-ceiling windows.

"No! No…no…no! Please!"

They kicked the glass. It shattered in a controlled burst, cold air whipping through the room like death entering.

Outside, the city blinked.

They didn't hesitate.

They lifted him, his heels scraping marble, and tossed him into the blackness.

Twenty-two floors down.

The scream cut through the night. The crash of bone and metal was louder.

Traffic swerved. People screamed. Phones came out.

Porscha stepped to the open window, hair whipping across her face.

Cory lit a cigar and passed it to her.

She puffed once, exhaled slow, then murmured, "He wanted to be known... now he's fuckin' headline news."

She turned away. The room still smelled like fear and blood.

Detective Boatwright pulled into the driveway of the quiet suburban home, the kind where the blinds are always halfway drawn and the silence feels a little too thick. She stepped out of the car, tension riding her shoulders, and walked up the front steps.

She knocked hard.

Waited.

Knocked again.

Nothing.

She pulled her phone and called Jessica.

Straight to voicemail.

Again.

Again.

"Come on, Jess..."

Boatwright let out a slow breath, walked back to her car, sat behind the wheel, and stared at the door like it might give her answers. She hit Detective Flowers' number.

He answered with urgency in his voice.

"You won't believe the body that just turned up."

Her brows furrowed. "What body?"

"Remember that judge who vanished almost ten months ago? Brad Smith?"

Boatwright straightened in her seat. "You talkin' about Judge Brad Smith? From the Emilio Sanchez case?"

"Yeah. Someone pulled him out of the East River. Wrapped in plastic, chained to two cinder blocks. Been there ten months easy. A chain he always wore is how he can tell it's him."

Boatwright closed her eyes. "You gotta be kidding me…"

"Wish I was. Somebody didn't just want him gone, they wanted him forgotten."

She took a slow breath. "I'm sitting outside Jessica's place right now. No answer at the door. Her phone's off. This whole thing's feelin' wrong."

There was a pause on his end. "You think it's connected?"

"I don't believe in coincidence anymore, Flowers."

"Go around back. Look through the window. See what's what."

"Alright," she said quietly, hanging up

Boatwright moved fast along the gravel path, flashlight in one hand, other near her sidearm. She reached the back window, leaned in close, shielding the glare with her palm as she pressed her face to the glass.

What she saw made her blood stop cold.

Jessica. Hanging in the middle of the living room.

Her body was still. Skin bloated, purple around the neck. The cord wrapped tight. Feet barely brushing the floor.

Three days gone.

Boatwright stumbled back, nearly losing her footing, then spun and ran.

CRACK!

Her foot shattered the door frame, splintering it open.

She rushed in, eyes burning, voice trembling as she dialed dispatch.

"Dispatch, this is Detective Boatwright—confirming a 10-54. I've got a deceased female victim, possibly suicide, possibly staged. Location is 6123 West Emerson. Time of death… at least seventy-two hours. I need backup, crime scene, and coroner now."

She swallowed hard, eyes locked on Jessica's lifeless body. The ceiling fan above it barely moved, casting slow, sad shadows on the walls.

She added, almost in a whisper, "And connect this to case file 2421B… Judge Brad Smith."

Chapter 14

The slaughterhouse had long been abandoned, tucked off a dirt road behind a forgotten truck yard. Its walls were stained with history—old blood, rust, the scent of rot buried deep in the concrete. It was perfect. Private. Quiet. The kind of place where things disappeared, and no one came looking.

Donnie stood near the center of the floor, dressed in black from collar to boot sole. He lit a cigarette with steady hands, the ember casting a brief glow across his sharp, unreadable face. A large, rusted drum sat nearby, filled halfway with acid—industrial grade. Lucchese didn't want a body. He wanted nothing.

Pauly's nephew showed up a few minutes late, buzzing with reckless energy, wiping sweat off his nose with the back of his hand. He was young—barely twenty-four—and stupid in the way only a street kid with false confidence could be.

"Unc's plug really hooked it up?" the kid asked, eyes dancing. "You serious?"

Donnie gave him a casual nod. "Yeah. Got a few bricks sittin' in storage. Figured I'd loop you in on this one. Time you started eatin' bigger."

The boy grinned like it was Christmas. "Hell yeah. Lemme get a taste first, though."

Donnie reached into a duffel on the table and tossed him a small bag of coke. The kid wasted no time, keying a line and sniffing hard.

Donnie moved in behind him quietly, like he was reaching for something else.

The first shot came sudden and clean, a hollow thud into the back of the kid's skull. He dropped instantly, face-first, arms bent beneath him like broken limbs.

Donnie didn't blink.

He fired again. Once. Twice. A fourth, right into the base of the neck. Blood pooled fast and thick across the cement.

He exhaled a slow drag from his cigarette and stared at the body for a long moment. No satisfaction. No regret. Just duty.

This wasn't about the kid.

It was about Pauly.

It was about what happens when loyalty breaks and blood spills.

Lucchese's voice echoed in his head. "You kill the future, not the past. You don't punish a man. You erase his legacy."

Donnie pulled on a pair of black gloves and dragged the body by its arms, leaving a streak of crimson across the floor. He lifted the corpse with a grunt and dumped it into the acid-filled drum. A hiss filled the room as flesh began to melt, bubbling violently.

The air thickened with smoke and the stench of decay. Donnie didn't flinch.

He stood there in silence, smoking calmly, eyes locked on the barrel until the last recognizable piece of the boy was gone.

Lucchese would be pleased.

No body.

No answers.

Just pain.

And Pauly? He'd feel it. In his soul. That was the point.

***

Red and blue lights pulsed across the front lawn, casting long, broken shadows against the white siding of Jessica's house. Yellow crime scene tape flapped in the breeze, stretched from porch post to mailbox, sealing off a tragedy that still didn't feel real.

Detective Flowers stood at the edge of the scene, jaw locked, arms folded across his chest. He'd seen bodies before—too many—but this one twisted something deep in his gut.

Not because of what was done.

But because of who it was.

Inside the house, more than twenty CSU officers moved in quiet rhythm. Cameras flashed. Evidence markers dotted the floor. A forensic tech dusted the stair banister while another carefully bagged fibers from the area near the beam where Jessica's body had been found hanging, suspended in cruel silence for three full days.

"She deserved better," came a voice beside him.

Flowers turned to see Detective Boatwright, her face pale, lips pressed thin. She looked exhausted—emotionally hollowed out.

"You were the one who found her," Flowers said.

Boatwright nodded slowly. "No answer at the door. Her phone went straight to voicemail. I had a bad feeling... you told me about Judge Smith, and I just..." She swallowed hard. "I looked through the back window and saw her. Just hanging there. Like some forgotten ornament in a room no one walks in anymore."

Flowers closed his eyes for a second. "You kicked in the front door?"

"I had to," she said, voice cracking. "Her body was stiff. Skin was already breaking down. She'd been dead three days, maybe more. The ME will confirm, but she wasn't just hanged. Someone staged it."

Flowers's brow furrowed. "What do you mean?"

Boatwright looked back at the house. "There were signs of a struggle. A chair overturned, rug bunched. Some bruising—defensive wounds. She fought. Hard. Whoever did this wanted it to look like suicide, but Jessica didn't go out like that."

Flowers sighed through his nose. "This ties back to Judge Brad Smith. No way it doesn't."

"Same people?" Boatwright asked.

"Same playbook," he said. "Judge gets pulled out of a lake, ten months dead. Now Jessica's found hanging. Both were talking about Trayvon and other judges."

Boatwright's hands curled into fists. "So, what now?"

Flowers looked toward the swarm of officers inside, then back at her.

"Now we follow the bodies," he said. "Because Trayvon's sending messages, and I need to know how loud he plans to get."

Boatwright nodded. "You think we'll find Frankie?"

Flowers stared at the horizon, jaw tight.

"If we don't find him soon," he said, "we'll be pulling another body out of another forgotten room."

Chapter 15

The headlines had stopped being shocking. Too many bodies. Too many secrets. Too many unanswered questions.

But tonight, this night, the air hung heavier. It was the kind of night where the television glowed like a silent judge in every living room. And on every screen across New York City, Channel 7's anchor Tamara Stone stared directly into the lens like she was looking through the glass and into people's souls.

"Good evening," she said, her voice a slow blade. "I'm Tamara Stone, and what we have tonight… you're not going to want to miss."

The screen behind her flickered with words no one ever wanted to hear.

BODY IN LAKE. JUDGE MISSING 10 MONTHS.

CANDIDATE KILLED.

NYPD SILENT.

The image snapped to live footage. A lake, quiet and dark. Blue lights shimmered off the water's surface. Crime scene tape flapped in the wind. Tamara's voice carried over the images.

"Former Judge Brad Smith's body was discovered yesterday afternoon, submerged in Lake Hollow—just outside the city. For ten months, his name was whispered in rumors. His disappearance had been labeled everything from suicide to sabotage. But now, we have confirmation. A body. A chain with the scales of justice. Blunt force trauma. And a silence deeper than the lake itself."

People in living rooms across the city turned up the volume. Something was happening. And the news wasn't letting it slide.

The scene changed again—this time to Brooklyn. A brownstone wrapped in yellow tape. Officers walked out, solemn and stone-faced. Onlookers wept behind barriers.

"Jessica Long," Tamara continued, "was found dead this morning. Hanging. No note. No forced entry. No sign of life for seventy-two hours before Detective Boatwright found her and called it in. Bruising around the neck suggests this wasn't suicide."

"Jessica wasn't just another name," Tamara said. "She served this city. She knew its dirt. She knew the politics. She knew who was really pulling strings behind closed doors. And now—she's gone."

Back at the Channel 7 studio, Tamara leaned forward on her desk. The cameras zoomed in. Her eyes were sharper than the script.

"This isn't coincidence," she said.

A new graphic rolled across the screen.

22ND FLOOR DEATH – MAYORAL CANDIDATE FOUND MURDERED

The anchor's voice dipped to a near whisper, every word perfectly enunciated.

"Cedric Harper, forty-four years old. Rising star. Family money. Political machine behind him. Was thrown off the penthouse suite balcony at Rosemont Towers—twenty-two stories above street level. Multiple sources claim a woman resembling Porscha Shields was seen entering the building hours before. Two men were with her. Surveillance footage is mysteriously missing."

Tamara paused. The tension was measured, sharpened, dangerous.

"The suite, by the way, was paid for by Cedric's cousin—Paul 'Pauly' Harper, one of his biggest backers. Now? Pauly's nowhere to be found."

A new package played. The footage was darker now—and more violent. Two stretchers. A body bag zipped. A crime scene in Queens.

"Just days earlier, Cedric's brother Devon Harper and Devon's wife Laila, were found murdered in their home. Execution-style. Two bullets each. Doors locked. No signs of robbery. Just a message. And now, Cedric is gone too. Three coffins in under five days."

By now, the ticker at the bottom of the screen was cycling through headlines faster than viewers could read.

"We asked the NYPD for comment. We asked the DA's office. We even reached out to federal agents assigned to the city's organized crime task force," Tamara said coldly. "And do you know what we got?"

The screen faded to black. Her voice continued.

"Nothing."

A moment passed. The screen came back to her face.

"This city is bleeding. In ten weeks, there have been over forty-seven unsolved homicides tied to either the legal system or political offices. These aren't random acts of violence. These are chess moves. And we're losing pieces fast."

***

Outside across the city every diner, bodega, and bar had the news on

In a Harlem barbershop, a group of men sat frozen mid-conversation. In a Staten Island deli, a mother stopped bagging groceries and just stared. In a luxury high-rise in Midtown, someone muted the volume and took out their phone. Texts began flying.

And inside a black Escalade somewhere in Brooklyn, a woman named Porscha smirked as the screen played in the dashboard.

"Now they talkin'."

But back on Channel 7, Tamara Stone leaned closer to the camera like she was about to confess something the city didn't want to hear.

"They're going to try to bury this. The bodies. The truth. Everything. But this story is bigger than them. Bigger than fear. And if they think a few headlines and some silence can shut this city up—then they haven't been paying attention."

She smiled once—just once.

"This is New York. And the truth always floats."

***

Pauly sat alone in his study, the kind of silence that felt like a scream crawling under his skin. The room smelled of leather and anger—old cigar smoke and new betrayal. Outside, the garden was still, but inside him, everything was moving too fast.

He lit a cigarette with shaking fingers and stared at the empty glass on the table in front of him.

His nephew—his blood—was gone.

And Cedric Harper? Dead. Thrown off the goddamn 22nd floor like garbage. No suspects. No answers. Just rumors and silence.

But Pauly didn't need a police report.

He knew.

Lucchese was behind it.

First Cedric. Then his nephew. No bodies, no witnesses, no messages.

That was the message.

Pauly slammed his fist down on the glass table, cracking it through the center.

His two men—Junebug and Ant—stood frozen by the door, watching Pauly boil.

"He ain't even tryin' to hide it," Pauly muttered, smoke curling from his mouth. "That muthafuckin' snake is making moves in the dark. Like I can't see."

Ant stepped forward, cautious. "We don't have proof. Not yet."

Pauly's eyes snapped up. "Proof? You want proof? Cedric Harper's blood is still on the damn penthouse floor. And my nephew's been gone three days. No word. You know him. He ain't the type to run off."

"He's dead," Junebug said quietly.

Pauly nodded once, slow and heavy. "Yeah. Yeah, he is."

Silence sat heavy in the room.

Ant glanced between the two. "So, what now?"

Pauly stood up, tossing the cigarette into the cracked ashtray.

"Now?" he said. "Now it's war."

The words didn't come out loud. They didn't need to. They sank in like bullets.

"Lucchese thinks he can chip away at me, piece by piece. Kill a politician I backed. Kill my own blood. Send a message without sending a word?" Pauly paced to the window. "But he don't know me. He don't know what I got lined up."

Ant blinked. "You talkin' retaliation?"

"I'm talkin' fire," Pauly said. "I'm talkin' takin' somethin' from him that'll echo. Somethin' that won't just hurt—it'll haunt. I want him to feel what I'm feelin' right now. I want him to wake up at night sweatin'."

Junebug shifted uncomfortably. "If you move now, it's gonna turn the streets into a bloodbath. The feds already poking around since Cedric died."

Pauly turned, eyes ice cold.

"Then let it rain."

The words cut the air like a straight razor.

"Tell every ear we got on the street to listen up. We don't move stupid—but we move heavy. I want Lucchese to feel the city shift under his feet."

Junebug nodded. "Understood."

Pauly sat back down slowly, resting his hands on the armrests like a king on a crumbling throne.

"Blood for blood. Body for body. He took mine. Now I take his."

***

Outside, the wind stirred the trees. The night held its breath.

And war crept in through the cracks.

Nestled behind a long, winding road guarded by iron gates and well-armed security, the Hillcrest Country Club wasn't the kind of place anyone stumbled into. The elite went there to hide in plain sight—politicians, judges, high-ranking law enforcement, and men whose names never made headlines but moved millions in silence.

The sun was beginning to set, casting an orange hue over the pristine golf course just beyond the wide glass windows. A private lounge, off-limits to regular members, sat tucked behind a mahogany-paneled wall. The room smelled of expensive cigars and old money. Inside, a round oak table gleamed under a low crystal chandelier. Scotch glasses clinked. The conversation was kept low and serious.

FBI Senior Chief Henry Goldwyn, in a tailored gray suit and polished demeanor, sat across from Judge Adem Miller and Mayor Michael Rakim.

Goldwyn sipped from his drink, then leaned forward, his voice steady but laced with urgency.

"They're moving," he said plainly. "Captain Lawson met with Detectives Boatwright and Flowers—yesterday. Behind closed doors, no paperwork trail. But the objective is clear. They're assembling a task force to bring down Porscha Shields."

Mayor Rakim raised an eyebrow but didn't react beyond that. Judge Miller took a slow pull from his cigar, blowing smoke toward the ceiling.

Goldwyn continued. "They want to hit her on RICO—racketeering, organized crime, multiple violent acts tied to Club Mercedes and the activity surrounding Harper's campaign. They think she's the hub... and they're not entirely wrong."

Rakim finally spoke. "She is the hub. But without her, everything falls apart. The streets? Chaos. Business? Paralyzed. And politics?" He gestured at himself and the judge. "We're exposed. You know what this means for us."

"I know," Goldwyn nodded. "That's why I came to you first."

Judge Miller leaned forward now, his eyes sharp behind wire-framed glasses. "Who authorized this investigation? The captain doesn't move without someone greenlighting it."

"I've traced whispers to the U.S. Attorney's Office," Goldwyn said. "They're eager to make a name. A high-profile woman, criminal empire, alleged political ties—hell, she's the perfect face for headlines and re-election campaigns. They don't care who she buries on the way down."

Rakim chuckled bitterly. "And I suppose they plan to throw some of us in the pit with her?"

Goldwyn's silence was answer enough.

Judge Miller sat back, letting it all sink in. "So... what are we saying here? Damage control? Interference? Or counterattack?"

"All of the above," Goldwyn said. "This isn't just about saving Porscha. It's about protecting all of us. If they start knocking on doors, digging into campaign contributions, court favors, and city contracts—" he looked pointedly at Rakim. "—we're all done."

Rakim set down his drink with a dull clink. "She won't go quietly. And she won't be caught off guard. But someone needs to give her the full picture. She trusts few people."

Miller nodded, tapping ash into a crystal tray. "Trayvon."

Goldwyn raised an eyebrow. "You think he can get through to her?"

"I know he can," Miller replied. "He's the only one she ever listens to when she's half a breath from war. And if we don't calm her down, redirect this heat, she'll start striking out before she understands who her real enemies are."

Rakim folded his arms. "So, what's the move? You want me to bring Trayvon in?"

"No," Judge Miller said, rising from his seat. "I'll talk to him myself. He trusts me more than he trusts the system. And he'll relay the message... directly."

Goldwyn stood with him. "Make sure he makes it crystal clear—this isn't just about her being arrested. It's about dismantling everything she built. They want to ruin her name, her legacy, and take anyone connected down with her."

"I'll make it clear," Miller said.

The three men stood in silence for a moment. Power, fear, and strategy thick in the air.

Goldwyn straightened his cufflinks. "If this goes sideways, you didn't hear it from me."

Miller gave a faint smirk. "I never do."

As Goldwyn left the lounge through a back corridor, Mayor Rakim leaned against the table, deep in thought.

Miller poured another glass of scotch. "Call Trayvon. Tonight. Tell him I need to speak. No delays."

Rakim nodded, then pulled out his phone.

Chapter 16

The sun stretched lazy fingers over the vineyard as Porscha sat beneath the private canopy at Vigna Verde, her sanctuary turned into a meeting ground. She looked untouchable—white designer slacks hugged her curves, a silky gold blouse tucked in at the waist, heels sharp enough to slice egos, and Cartier shades shielding eyes colder than the Chardonnay in her glass.

Rakim stood behind her chair like a silent weapon, scanning every inch of the secluded terrace for danger—even though he knew the real threat was seated in front of her.

Mr. Wright—Escobar Sanchez's legal bloodhound—sat down slowly, briefcase between his legs, that usual self-satisfied grin tucked in the corner of his mouth. Porscha didn't offer a smile, a handshake, or a fake greeting.

"Let's skip the performance," she said flatly. "How much of the mess am I supposed to clean?"

He clicked open the briefcase and laid out a single document on the table. "Two hundred million. Your share."

She snorted softly and took a sip of wine. "He wants five hundred cleaned total, right?"

"Correct," Wright nodded. "You and your father were both selected because of your networks, resources, and… your history with discretion."

Porscha tilted her glass. "He didn't select us. He needed us."

Wright hesitated, then nodded. "Fair enough. The first hundred is already prepped for movement. Rakim will find encrypted account data on the flash drive inside this folder."

Rakim leaned forward, retrieved the drive, and slid it into his jacket without a word.

"Once you move that," Wright continued, "the next hundred gets released. And then—your father will handle the remainder."

Porscha raised an eyebrow. "He know that?"

"He will," Wright said. "I'm heading to see him next. And I've got something for him. A personal delivery from Escobar Sanchez himself."

Porscha set her wine glass down slowly.

"A package?"

Wright nodded. "Locked briefcase. Combination only your father knows. Sanchez said it's… a reminder."

She leaned forward slightly. "You sure you want to be the one bringing him 'reminders?' He's not as diplomatic as I am."

Wright straightened his tie. "I'm just the messenger."

"No," Porscha said, standing. "You're the liability."

She walked around the table, heels tapping lightly against the stone, and stopped just short of him.

"You tell Sanchez this gets done on my schedule. Not his. If I smell even a hint of funny business with this money…"

She tapped her nail against her wine glass, the sharp ting echoing like a warning.

"I'm not calling my father to fix it. I'm calling someone to bury him."

Wright didn't blink. Just gathered his things, nodded once to Rakim, and walked off like he had a death sentence tucked inside his briefcase.

When he was gone, Porscha exhaled deeply and looked out across the endless vines.

"Escobar's playing chess with landmines," she muttered. "And he thinks my father's gonna let him call the shots."

Rakim raised an eyebrow. "You think he knows who he's dealing with?"

She smirked. "He's about to."

***

Trayvon sat alone in the dim backroom of Le Serpent, the underground cigar lounge hidden beneath the old church. A single Cuban burned slow between his fingers. The smoke swirled up toward the stained-glass ceiling, flickering with candlelight.

The door creaked open.

Mr. Wright stepped inside with the same confident calm that made men hate him or fear him—sometimes both. In his hand, he carried a small, black velvet box.

"Trayvon," he greeted, voice as smooth as ever.

Trayvon didn't rise. He didn't even blink. "Mr. Wright."

They exchanged a cold silence before Wright placed the box gently on the mahogany table and sat across from him.

"I assume this is business?" Trayvon asked.

"Strictly," Wright replied. "From Escobar Sanchez. A message… and a gift."

Trayvon tapped the ashes of his cigar into a crystal tray. "Go on."

Mr. Wright unlatched the box and slowly turned it toward Trayvon.

Inside lay a bloody napkin. Wrapped tightly inside it, a severed finger. Still fresh. Still warm. And around that finger—a thick, rose gold pinky ring embedded with a dark emerald stone, unmistakable.

Trayvon's jaw clenched. His eyes narrowed.

He knew that ring. It belonged to Diego Sanchez— Escobar's only son. The same son who'd recently sent four hundred kilos of high-grade cocaine to Trayvon's ports… unannounced. Dangerous. Disrespectful.

"You want to explain this?" Trayvon asked, voice like gravel over fire.

Wright slid a small, folded note across the table. Trayvon picked it up, unfolded it, and read silently.

"The four hundred kilos my son sent you came with a blood price. I know you didn't ask for them—so his finger was the price. Remember... when a dog growls at its owner, it's challenging him. When our children undermine us, they challenge us. Make no mistake—I love my son. But next time, I'll be sending you his head. To show you family is just blood in the veins... Loyalty keeps you walking among them."

Trayvon lowered the note with his eyes still fixed on the box.

He didn't speak for a long moment. Then, finally, "Escobar sent a message," he said. "One hell of a message."

"He wanted you to know where he stands," Wright replied. "The boy acted on ego. He paid the price. But the product? It's still yours to move."

Trayvon let out a slow breath through his nose. "This some Roman Empire shit."

Wright smirked. "Sometimes the throne bleeds to stay clean."

Trayvon reached forward and closed the box with a soft click. "Tell Escobar... I hear him. Loud and clear."

Wright stood and adjusted his cuffs. "He figured you would."

As he turned to leave, Trayvon called after him.

"Oh—and Wright?"

"Yes?"

"Next time he sends a part of someone..." Trayvon's eyes burned like fire under coal. "...tell him to pick a smaller finger. That emerald ain't my style."

Wright chuckled softly, then vanished behind the velvet curtain.

Trayvon sat in the smoke and silence, the box still in front of him, and muttered under his breath, "Blood for product. Sons for shipments. This world's already on fire."

Chapter 17

Detective Sherri Boatwright was in mid-argument with her lieutenant when her radio crackled.

"Unit 31, we have a confirmed explosion on Westside Avenue—address matches… your mother's residence."

Her heart skipped.

She dropped the radio and sprinted for her cruiser. Red and blue lights painted her tear-streaked face as she tore through the streets like a ghost on fire. When she arrived, the crowd had already gathered. Neighbors screamed. Firemen yelled. The sky was black with smoke.

And the house?

Gone.

Her mother's porch swing—the one she sat on as a kid—was a mangled mess of wood and chain lying halfway in the street. Sherri's knees gave out. She crawled forward on hands and knees, screaming for her mother.

That's when she saw the second body.

"Who is that?" she yelled, grabbing a medic by the collar. "Who?"

The medic hesitated then looked down.

"Your father… he… he was inside."

Sherri didn't even know he was in town.

· They had been trying to fix things.

She collapsed, sobbing, fists pounding the concrete, blood mixing with the tears on her face. Her badge fell to the ground.

And across the street, parked in a sleek black SUV, Porscha sat with the window halfway down, puffing on a cigar like it was just another Thursday.

"Play with me again, bitch," she whispered.

***

Detective Elijah Flowers had always been the calm one. Tactical. Rational. Emotionless, even.

But nothing could prepare him for what he saw when he came home that night.

The door was unlocked.

The house was still.

He called out, "Tay? Eli? Daddy's home!"

No answer.

He stepped into the living room. His daughter's backpack was still on the couch. His son's shoes were by the door. A fresh plate of cookies sat on the table untouched.

Something was wrong.

His instincts kicked in.

He rushed to the kitchen. That's when he saw it.

The box.

Wrapped in newspaper. Duct-taped with surgical precision.

The note was written in blood-red ink on black paper.

"Come after me again… and I'll send they fucking heads to you in a box."

He couldn't breathe.

He ripped the box open, screaming.

Empty.

But the sock on the floor. The broken toy under the table. The cereal still in their bowls…

They were taken.

His knees hit the tile. The room spun. He clutched the floor like he was trying to hold onto the earth itself.

His phone buzzed. A single image came through.

His two children. Blindfolded. Hands tied. Sitting quietly on a dirty mattress.

And a caption underneath… "You had one job. Walk away."

***

Captain Marcus Lawson thought he was untouchable.

As he strutted out of the precinct in full uniform, he paused at the top of the stairs. The sun was just starting to set,

He took a long sip of coffee and glanced down at his phone, texting his wife.

"On my way, love. Pasta tonight?"

Then the first shot hit.

His body jerked violently, the coffee cup launching from his hand.

The second shot followed a heartbeat later, striking dead center.

He stumbled down two steps before collapsing in front of the glass doors of the station—his blood staining the stone like a warning.

His eyes stayed open, wide, frozen in shock.

Officers screamed.

Cops scrambled.

Cameras captured everything.

And from an anonymous number, Porscha sent a group text to Flowers, Boatwright, and every major in the precinct.

"Your King is dead. Stop playing with fire that thin line of ice you was walking on just broke."

Porscha didn't need to yell to make her presence known.

She didn't need a courtroom or a badge.

She had fear. She had reputation. She had power.

Rakim stood behind her as she stared out the 40th floor window, glass of dark rum in her hand, silk robe flowing like royalty.

"They pushed, Porscha," Rakim said. "You sure you wanna finish this?"

She didn't even flinch.

"They kept testing me," she said calmly. "I told them. I warned them. This ain't a game."

She turned to him.

"Trayvon told me about that little meeting. Internal Affairs. Trying to link me to Club Mercedes. Trying to flip my people. That was their move."

She sat down in her white leather chair, lit her cigar, and smiled like a woman who already written the final chapter.

"Well now... this is mine."

She sent the messages out one by one. Gave the order. Sat back and watched the city burn from above.

The detectives. The captain. The department.

All cracking beneath her feet.

They were warned.

Now they were witnesses to what happens when the queen moves first.

***

The warehouse sat abandoned at the far end of Queens, where even the rats were scared to roam. Its rusted steel doors groaned with age, and the wind whispered through broken windows like the voices of ghosts. It was the kind of place made for secrets—out of sight, out of mind.

Trayvon walked in slow, quiet steps, his Glock weighing heavily beneath his hoodie. He didn't come to start a war—but he was ready to walk out of one. The air inside the warehouse was damp, metallic. A single hanging bulb above flickered like it might die at any moment.

Standing beneath it was Escobar Sanchez's only son.

He wasn't dressed like cartel royalty tonight—no gold, no designer anything. Just black jeans, a hoodie, and rage. His left hand was wrapped in a deep red bandage. The blood had soaked through, even though the wound was a day old.

Trayvon stopped a few feet away, eyes sweeping the warehouse.

"You alone?" he asked.

The son's voice was low. Flat. "If I wasn't, you wouldn't have made it past the door."

Trayvon gave a nod and stepped forward.

"You called this meet. Speak."

Sanchez's son slowly peeled back part of the cloth wrapped around his hand. A jagged stump stared back at Trayvon—his pinky finger, gone. The cut was rough. Personal.

"He did this," the son said quietly. "My father."

Trayvon said nothing. Just stared.

"You know why?" the son continued. "Because I sent you four hundred extra keys."

Trayvon's brow creased. "You did that outta loyalty. You said it was a show of good faith."

"It was," he snapped. "You and your daughter risked everything to get me out of that mess. Interpol was about to drag me back to Spain in chains. If you hadn't made those moves with your daughter and contacts—"

"We did it because you're an ally," Trayvon cut in.

"Exactly," the son hissed. "But to my father? That was betrayal. He told me I showed too much loyalty to outsiders. He said I was getting soft."

Trayvon stepped closer, voice low. "He cut your finger off for showing loyalty?"

"No," the son corrected, eyes dark. "He cut it off because I stood beside you. Because I believe in what you and your daughter are building in New York. He sees that as weakness."

He looked away for a moment, chest rising with emotion. "He's scared of your daughter. Of how people are starting to respect her name in rooms they used to fear his. She's young, she's ruthless, and she's fair. That's power. And power scares Escobar."

Trayvon's jaw tightened.

"He thinks I'm turning against him. And maybe I am," the son said, facing him again. "Because the man I once called a father ain't the same anymore. He's paying Homeland Security and federal agencies to clean up his enemies while hiding behind you to wash his blood money. He wants everything fast. He's reckless. No more honor, no more patience—just paranoia and control."

Trayvon stared long and hard.

"And now you want to take his place?"

The son's voice cracked slightly—but not from fear.

"I want to survive. If he did this to me," he raised the bandaged hand again, "what you think he'll do to you? To your daughter? She's not just a threat to him—she's a replacement."

Trayvon's silence stretched like a noose between them.

"If we don't take him out," the son added, stepping forward, "he'll kill everything we've built. I know it. You know it."

Trayvon's eyes never left his.

"You understand what you're asking me to do?"

"Yes," the son said without hesitation. "Help me kill Escobar Sanchez. Help me burn the old empire down before it kills us both."

Trayvon reached into his coat and pulled out a single black glove. He tossed it toward him.

"No mistakes. No second chances."

The son caught the glove in his wounded hand and looked Trayvon in the eye.

"I've already bled for this."

Trayvon nodded once.

"Then let's make him bleed next."

Above them, the single bulb finally gave out.

Darkness took over.

But the war had just begun.

Chapter 18

The warehouse on the outskirts of Jersey was cold, dark, and humming with violence. Fluorescent lights flickered overhead like a heartbeat about to flatline. Tables stacked with AKs, M16s, shotguns, crates of ammunition, explosives, and bulletproof vests. This wasn't preparation. This was premeditation.

Lucchese stood at the center of it all, dressed in black, rage wrapped in skin. His face was hard and his knuckles were cracked from pounding tables and putting holes in walls. His voice echoed like thunder.

"This ain't no negotiation," he snarled. "This is genocide. I want Pauly wiped out like he never fucking existed."

His top lieutenants—Gino, Tommy Two-Times, and Ricco—loaded their weapons, their hands moving like this was second nature. Death had become a routine.

Ricco zipped a body bag closed with no body in it yet. "You want us to bring back heads or just make 'em disappear?"

Lucchese lit a cigarette with trembling fingers. "Burn 'em. Burn their fuckin' souls. I want smoke rising outta Pauly's territory like the gates of Hell just opened."

Behind him, trucks were being loaded—fully armored SUVs, sedans with no plates, vans with hidden compartments. Blood was coming, and Lucchese wanted to drown in it.

"Every bullet's a message. Every body's a warning. Let Pauly know—there's no mercy left in me."

He raised a rifle, aimed it at a wall, and fired five rounds into a crooked family portrait of Sammy the Don.

"Let's go to war."

***

On the opposite side of town, Pauly sat in a steel-reinforced basement. Dim lights. Concrete walls. War maps of city blocks with pins jammed into every hotspot. Around him, his inner circle suited up with flak vests, duffels full of guns, black gloves, and murder in their eyes.

"He wants blood?" Pauly spat. "Good. I got more than enough to give."

Pauly's right-hand man, Buck, checked the magazine on a gold-plated 9mm. "Word is, Lucchese's comin' with everything."

Pauly looked up with eyes that hadn't blinked in hours. "Then I'll meet him halfway. We goin' door to door. Anybody even look connected to him? Drop 'em."

There was no room for second thoughts. Lucchese had made it personal. Pauly still mourned the disappearance of his nephew—no body, no funeral, just a void. That kind of hurt made men into monsters.

He opened a safe, pulled out a sawed-off shotgun with "FAMILY FIRST" engraved on the barrel. "If this is my last stand, I'm takin' the whole goddamn block with me."

The men nodded.

They weren't getting ready for a battle. They were preparing for a massacre.

The smell of fish and betrayal filled the air. Nick the Boss sat behind the counter, skin pale, eyes sharp, cutting through lies like fillet knives. Big Pete walked in, nervous sweat dripping down his temple, fedora tilted to hide fear.

"I need to talk to you, Nick," Pete said.

Nick didn't move. Just stared. "You smell that?"

Pete hesitated. "What?"

"Smells like rats. You smell it?"

"I ain't no—"

"Don't even finish that fuckin' lie," Nick snapped, standing. "Lucchese wants you dead. Pauly wants you dead. Even Trayvon sent feelers out on your name."

Pete's lip trembled. "I didn't mean for it to go that far—"

"You never do," Nick said. "You think informin' makes you important. But it just makes you food."

Pete pleaded, voice cracking. "I came to you for help. I got no one else."

Nick stepped closer, put his hand on Pete's shoulder, then leaned in. "You ever seen what a man looks like after a thousand crab bites in cold water?"

Pete froze.

Nick leaned back. "Leave the market. Don't look back."

Pete turned to go, shoulders shaking.

Nick stared after him.

We never saw Pete again.

***

Detective Boatwright sat with her head in her hands, eyes swollen from crying. Across from her, Detective Flowers punched the wall until his knuckles bled.

Captain Lawson was dead.

Boatwright's father—executed.

Flowers' children—gone without a trace.

The room was dark. Not just in lighting, but in feeling. There was no justice left. Just revenge.

"I told you," Boatwright whispered, "we should've killed them all when we had the chance."

Flowers sat down, face pale, trembling. "I don't even know if my kids are alive."

Boatwright stood up and slammed her badge on the table. "This badge means nothing now. Nothing."

The silence was so thick it could've suffocated them.

They were no longer detectives. They were ghosts—carrying the weight of bodies not buried.

***

Homeland Security was supposed to be the clean side of crime.

But Escobar Sanchez sat across from a suited agent, briefcase open. Stacks of cash. Two envelopes. Names. Locations.

"I want them eliminated," Escobar said, coldly. "No questions."

The agent took the money without blinking. "We'll handle it."

Across the room, Emilio Sanchez—his son—watched, disgusted.

"You're paying the government to fight your battles now?" Emilio sneered.

Escobar didn't flinch. "This is how kings stay kings."

Emilio shook his head. "You're not a king. You're a coward."

Their eyes locked. Father and son. One playing chess. The other ready to flip the board.

***

A hidden location in upstate New York. A mansion built like a fortress. Porscha and Trayvon sat in front of a roaring fireplace, two glasses of blood-red wine on the table between them.

This wasn't a casual conversation.

This was the purge.

"The judge?" Trayvon said. "I pulled him from the lake myself. Left his body on the shore. Made sure he was found."

Porscha nodded. "Jessica?"

"Strung up in her living room. Made it look like suicide. Cops bought it."

"And Sammy the Don?"

Porscha smiled darkly. "Paris, Corey, and Realz. I gave the order. They carried it out. No loose ends."

Trayvon exhaled, pride and fear mixing like smoke and oxygen. "And Cedric Harper?"

"Necessary," she said, "just like you said, make it loud. He was talking too much. Death was at his doorstep, and he opened the door, and I walked in."

There was a long pause. The weight of their sins filled the room.

"We laundered more money in six months than the Colombians did in a year," Trayvon said. "We're not a family anymore, Porscha. We're a goddamn army."

Porscha stood up, her eyes burning.

"No, Daddy. We're not an army."

He looked at her.

She walked to the window and stared out at the forest beyond.

"We're a virus. We infect everything we touch. And when the world finally notices—we'll already be in their bloodstream."

Trayvon didn't respond. He knew she was right.

Porscha lit a cigar. Her voice was low, final, deadly.

"You want a title? Here's one for the books…"

She turned.

"I'm the end of peace. I'm what comes after mercy dies."

Chapter 19

The call came from a blocked number.

"One hour. Manhattan. 12th and Hawthorne. Come alone."

No explanation. No time for backup. Just a voice dripping in steel. Detective Flowers knew who it was the moment the call disconnected—and he knew this was about Alex and Alexis.

Now, parked outside an abandoned meatpacking warehouse tucked beneath the edge of lower Manhattan, he stepped into the darkness. The building sagged under the weight of its own decay—rusted beams, shattered glass, streaks of old blood staining the concrete floor. Every creak sounded like a death threat.

He moved slowly, his hand near his weapon, heart pounding.

Then came the purr of a high-end engine. A black Maybach slid through the shadows like a serpent. It stopped without sound. The back door opened.

Porscha stepped out.

Draped in a tailored trench coat from Paris, stilettos that clicked like gunshots, and a necklace that glittered like sharpened diamonds, she was the picture of high-class danger. Her presence didn't walk into a room—it possessed it.

She didn't speak right away. She just stared, lips slightly parted, eyes unreadable. When she finally spoke, her voice came out low and precise, like a scalpel.

"You got a lot of fucking nerve, Flowers."

He tensed as one of her men stepped forward, holding Alexis gently in his arms. Behind him, Alex walked out under his own strength, scared but unbroken. The detective's knees hit the ground before he could stop them, arms open.

His babies. Alive.

"They'll live," Porscha said, "for now."

The children were guided toward a black Escalade idling behind the Maybach. They climbed in, confused, silent. The doors locked with a heavy clunk.

Porscha moved in closer. Her heels echoed across the wet concrete, stopping just inches from his face.

"You hear that?" she whispered.

Flowers looked around.

Silence.

"Exactly. No traffic. No lights. No cameras. If I wanted to end all three of you tonight… no one would hear your screams."

His voice cracked as he stood. "Please… I just—"

"Shhh." She pressed a manicured finger to his lips. "You think I'm some street bitch? Because you wear a badge, you think you can play in my world?"

She stepped even closer, breath brushing his cheek.

"Alex and Alexis almost saw their last sunrise. You hear me?" She tapped his chest over his heart. "The ice you were walking on? It's broken, baby. You're drowning."

He swallowed hard. "What do you want?"

"You work for me now. Not the NYPD. Not IA. Not God. Me."

"I can't—"

"You will," she snapped, venom coating every syllable. "Because the next time you hesitate? They won't come back. And you'll live long enough to bury two caskets."

The weight of her words dropped on him like a guillotine. She leaned in closer, almost affectionate now.

"Judge Smith… found bloated in a lake."

She paused.

"Jessica… hanged from her ceiling like overripe fruit."

Another pause.

"Captain Lawson. One to the neck, three to the chest."

And then she stared deep into his eyes as her voice dipped into a whisper.

"Cedric Harper? Flew off the twenty-second floor like trash in the wind."

His lips parted, but no sound came out.

"You still think I won't kill yours?" she asked. "Killing's in my blood. It's my birthright."

He flinched.

She smiled.

"This is how it goes. You lie for me. You cover my shadows. You keep your mouth shut when IA starts sniffing. And in return?" She arched a brow.

"You get to tuck your kids in at night."

He looked down, trembling. She took one step back, just enough to deliver her final words.

"This ain't a negotiation, Detective. This is an offer you can't refuse."

She turned away. The Maybach door opened like it knew her soul. Before stepping in, she paused and threw her voice back over her shoulder.

"Cross me again… and you'll need three graves. One for each of them… and one for your pride."

The car door closed. The Maybach glided off into the fog like a ghost with unfinished business.

Flowers stood frozen, the chill of her presence still clinging to his bones. His badge weighed heavier than it ever had before—because now, it didn't stand for justice.

It stood for silence.

And he belonged to Porscha.

The night air hung thick with salt, fish, and betrayal.

***

Big Pete stumbled out of the fish market, wiping his hands on his shirt not knowing it would be the last thing he'd ever touch. The sharp slap of footsteps echoed behind him— too many, too heavy, too sure. He didn't even have time to turn before a pipe smashed into the back of his knee, sending him crashing to the pavement.

"Fuck!" Pete screamed, curling in on himself. Another blow came down—then another. A bat slammed into his ribs, cracking them like twigs. A crowbar bit into his spine. His screams drowned beneath the grunts and cursing of men who once sat at tables with him, laughed with him, toasted life with him. The very same men were now ending his.

They didn't stop. They didn't let up. It wasn't just a beating—it was a message. The steel, the wood and the fists, they were all delivering the same truth. There's no coming back from betrayal.

Blood trailed behind them as they dragged his limp, barely breathing body through the mud, past the tree line, to a clearing where a fresh grave waited like it had been expecting him.

The moonlight hit the open dirt just right—made it look deeper, darker. The kind of hole you don't crawl out of.

Then he heard it, those slow, deliberate steps. Shoes crunching the gravel. Italian leather kissed the dirt like death itself was walking toward him.

Nick the Boss.

Not the man he remembered in cigars and smiles, but a storm of silence and fury. His black coat danced in the wind. His face… tight. His hands… trembling. And his eyes… his eyes were full of fire, pain, and history.

Nick knelt beside him. Looked at him like a brother, a ghost, and a traitor all at once.

"Twenty fuckin' years," Nick whispered. His voice was raw. Cracked. "Twenty fuckin' years, we was side by side."

Pete coughed, blood spilling from his lips. "Nick... please, I didn't—"

Nick's hand shot out, snatching Pete by the collar, dragging him halfway up out the mud.

"Shut the fuck up!" Nick roared, slamming him back down. "You didn't? You didn't know that fed was wearing a wire? You didn't know your weak-ass lips got half the family indicted? You didn't know your testimony got the Castellani twins locked up and put my goddamn nephew on the run?"

Pete cried now, sputtering through blood and regret. "I didn't mean—"

"You didn't mean?" Nick's voice cracked again, but this time with something closer to heartbreak. He stood up slowly. Wiped his face with a trembling hand. "We was brothers, Pete. You understand that? Not by blood—but by everything that matters."

Nick reached inside his coat and pulled out the .357 Magnum. Chrome kissed by moonlight.

"A soldier dies once..." Nick muttered, stepping forward, "...but a coward dies a thousand deaths."

Pete sobbed. "Nick, please..."

Nick looked down at him for a long time. So long it felt like the earth itself paused to listen.

"You know what I realized?" Nick said, voice low and broken. "You didn't just rat on us. You buried every memory we ever had. Every laugh, every job, every time I vouched for you—you turned that into evidence."

The hammer on the revolver clicked back.

Nick's hand shook. Not from fear. But from loss.

His eyes welled with tears, but his aim never wavered.

"You didn't just betray the mob," he said, barely above a whisper. "You betrayed me."

Then he leaned in, whispered the last words Big Pete would ever hear.

"There's no forgiveness in this life. Only balance."

The gunshot echoed through the trees, bounced off the stone walls of the city beyond, and sank into the bones of anyone who ever knew loyalty.

Big Pete's body dropped into the grave.

Nick stood over it, chest heaving, face soaked in tears.

He didn't say a word after that.

He just walked away… slower than he came.

Behind him, dirt was shoveled over what was once a brother, now just a lesson.

A soldier dies once.

A coward dies a thousand deaths.

But a rat?

A rat only dies once.

But it better be loud enough for the whole world to hear it.

***

The Bronx was lit with gunfire.

Smoke curled into the air like the city itself was exhaling death. The corners of 138th and Willis Avenue turned into a battlefield—bodies falling into busted-up pavement, bullets ricocheting off brick and metal.

Pauly's men had come deep—four cars strong, AKs, MAC-10s, and blood in their eyes. But Lucchese had been waiting. He'd turned the block into a trap. Shooters on rooftops, snipers in abandoned apartments, shadows hiding behind trash bins and parked vans.

When the first car rolled up, it was met with a rainstorm of bullets. Glass shattered. Metal screamed. Brains painted backseats.

"Down! Get down!" someone yelled, but it didn't matter. The ambush was merciless.

Pauly dove behind a car, firing his pistol blindly into the smoke. "Move up! Take that building!"

But his men were already falling. Rico took a headshot behind the mailbox, Vince was lit up crossing the street, and Ant screamed as his leg got torn apart.

Lucchese stepped through the chaos like he was walking through a memory. Calm, tailored coat flowing behind him, eyes locked forward, face blank as a coffin lid.

"Pauly!" he shouted over the roar. "You should've stayed in your fucking lane fat fuck! You ain't think we was going to find out you hit Porscha's club? It's because of you Sammy is fucking dead. You made that call, but I also made a few calls, you piece of shit."

Pauly ducked behind a staircase, reloading with shaky hands. "Come out and fight me, you snake!"

Lucchese smiled darkly, lifted his silenced pistol, and dropped one of Pauly's soldiers from across the street—one shot, right through the temple. "I am fighting you. I've been fighting you since the day you betrayed Sammy."

Pauly's eyes narrowed. Blood dripped down the side of his face. "I ain't betray no one!"

Lucchese motioned to his crew—three masked soldiers moved in, laying fire on what was left of Pauly's last men. Screams rang out. One was still twitching when they stomped his skull in.

Within minutes... it was over.

Bodies laid out like broken statues, blood staining snowdrifts and sidewalks. Sirens wailed in the far distance, but none of these men planned on sticking around to explain.

Lucchese walked toward Pauly, who was on his knees, panting, blood bubbling from a gut wound. His gun was empty. His world was ending.

Lucchese looked down at him, cold and patient. "You remember your sister's boy?"

Pauly's eyes widened. "Don't—don't you say it—"

"I had him killed." Lucchese crouched down. "Your nephew begged. Cried. He didn't deserve it. But you did. So, I made sure his body never touched a grave."

Pauly's scream was guttural, inhuman.

Lucchese leaned closer, his voice venom.

"The streets don't forget betrayal… but I don't forgive it either."

One shot.

Right between the eyes.

Pauly's head snapped back and slammed into the pavement.

Lucchese stood, holstered the pistol, and turned toward his men.

"Burn every car. Wipe the street clean. Let The Bronx know who owns this concrete now."

As they moved in silence, fires lit behind them—blazing wrecks that glowed like hell had opened its mouth.

Lucchese never looked back.

***

The moon hovered like a cold eye in the sky, casting silver shadows over the open waters. A luxury yacht drifted across the dark surface, its lights low, its music silent. The gentle lap of waves against the hull was the only rhythm playing tonight.

Escobar Sanchez sat on the deck's upper level, reclined in a deep leather chair, barefoot, wearing linen pants and an open silk shirt. A thick cigar burned slowly between his fingers, the smoke curling like a ghost above his head. He sipped from a crystal flute filled with Armand de Brignac champagne, its golden hue catching the moonlight.

He was at peace—unaware the night was no longer his.

"You ever notice," Escobar said, voice heavy with pride and age, "how on a chessboard, the king moves only one space at a time, but the game still revolves around him?"

Across from him stood his son, Emilio Sanchez. Younger, leaner, fire in his blood, betrayal in his eyes. He wasn't holding a glass. He was holding back rage.

"You always think you're the king, Papa," Emilio spat. "But you forgot—kings fall too."

Escobar grinned, not out of joy, but the arrogance of a man who believed the world owed him reverence. "Everything I did was survival. The police, the dirty favors, the arrangements... those were calculated sacrifices. Your uncle? He was reckless. He nearly had us buried under indictments and bullets."

"You had rivals killed by the government!" Emilio's voice cracked through the air like a whip. "You sold our soul to gringos. You cut off my finger, your own son's, in the name of loyalty. And you threatened her—Trayvon's daughter—because she saw through your bullshit."

Escobar leaned forward, eyes narrowing. "That girl was a liability. Trayvon? A pawn. You think loyalty runs the streets of New York? No, fear does. I built this empire, boy. You think your fire, your emotions, make you a man? I built men. I made Trayvon. I gave him the pipeline. The ports. The protection."

A third voice echoed from the darkness.

"You made a mistake."

Escobar's face froze.

From the shadows at the bow of the boat, Trayvon emerged like death wearing designer. All-black suit tailored sharp enough to cut wind, leather gloves gripping the silenced pistol at his side. The moonlight didn't touch him, it respected him.

He walked slowly, each step hollow on the wooden deck. Behind him, the city skyline flickered far in the distance, indifferent.

"You disrespected my daughter," Trayvon said calmly, leveling the gun. "You threatened her life over your own fear. You disrespected your own son, mutilated him to prove a point that no longer matters. And worst of all—you disrespected the game."

Escobar stood now, his body stiff, but not trembling. He met Trayvon's gaze with that old bravado, the kind only men who'd buried enemies and paid off governments knew.

"I made you, Trayvon. Everything you have, your seat at the table, your name—came from me. And this is how you repay me?"

Trayvon's eyes didn't flinch. "I am who I am. I was who I was… before I ever met you."

Click.

Pfft. Pfft. Pfft.

Three shots, silenced, but thunderous in meaning.

The rounds struck Escobar dead center in the chest. His glass fell first, shattering on the deck and splashing expensive champagne across his bare feet. His body followed, staggering back like a crumbling monument before he fell over the rail.

Splash.

Only two people heard it—Trayvon and Emilio.

The yacht didn't stop. It cruised forward, engine humming beneath them like a lullaby. The dark water swallowed the kingpin without remorse.

Silence reigned.

Trayvon turned toward Emilio, the barrel of his gun lowering. Emilio didn't flinch. Their eyes met in a cold agreement—revenge had been served.

"You knew what tonight was," Trayvon said, voice low.

Emilio nodded slowly, jaw tight. "He made me choose. Between him… and what was right."

Trayvon looked out over the water, lips tight.

"We're not right. None of us. But he forgot—this game ain't about kings anymore. It's about players who know how to move in silence."

Emilio exhaled.

Trayvon walked to the lower deck, disappearing once more into the dark.

Above, the stars blinked as if bearing witness. Below, the waves devoured the memory of Escobar Sanchez.

And the yacht kept gliding, smooth and silent... toward a new future drenched in blood, power, and reckoning.

Chapter 20

The weight of war had settled into Porscha's bones. The city was bleeding on every corner, and Detective Boatwright was becoming more than a thorn—she was a blade aiming straight for Porscha's empire. There was no shaking her. No threatening her. No bribing her. Every time they silenced a problem, Boatwright returned, hungrier, angrier, fueled by revenge and personal pain. Her eyes no longer saw the law—they saw blood.

Porscha leaned on the balcony rail of her penthouse, a velvet robe loosely tied around her waist, the wind catching her silk nightgown underneath. A Cuban cigar burned slow between her fingers. Behind her, Manhattan glittered like a diamond graveyard.

She had made her decision. There was no other way

"End it," she whispered into her burner phone.

Corey didn't respond. He didn't have to.

***

The sky was dark gray, thunderclouds building in the distance like nature was holding its breath. Mourners in black scattered through the cemetery grounds, umbrellas opening as light rain began to fall. Bagpipes played faintly in the distance, as if the sound mourned more than just Lawson—it mourned the last bit of order.

Detective Boatwright stood alone, her face stoic, black shades hiding the storm in her eyes. Her coat whipped in the wind as she walked slowly across the cracked concrete toward her unmarked vehicle. She knew Lawson's death wasn't random. She knew Porscha was pulling strings from her tower like some untouchable god. But Boatwright wasn't afraid. She had already buried too much to care about her own life. She just wanted justice.

She got in her car, yanked the door shut, and as she reached for the ignition— the motorcycle pulled up to the side door. Corey pointed the Glock 9 at her face and all you heard was the echo of the gun blast.

Two clean shots to the head.

Glass shattered. Blood painted the side window.

Her body slumped forward over the steering wheel. Horn blaring.

The motorcycle peeled off into the mist, tires screeching, engine screaming like a banshee, vanishing into the rainy blur of city streets. As other police officers were running to Detective Boatwright's car, Detective Flowers knew it was over, and she was dead. He never ran to the car because he knew Porscha sent her shooters at Detective Boatwright. This wasn't a message, this was personal and another piece on the chess board Porscha just moved.

***

Porscha didn't flinch. She watched the skyline as the news broke across her burner screen.

"Detective Boatwright was gunned down outside funeral service. Suspect fled the scene. No arrests have been made."

A small smirk pulled at her lips. The cigar burned slowly between her fingers, a long ash curling at the end.

"She should've walked away," she whispered to herself.

She turned and disappeared inside the suite, closing the balcony door behind her.

***

The waves were restless that night, the water choppy and silver under a pale moon. A fisherman named Rob, middle-aged and quiet, tugged at his nets when he saw something strange floating near the side of his small boat. At first, he thought it was debris—until the figure moved.

"Jesus Christ…" Rob muttered, yanking the man aboard.

It was Escobar Sanchez. Barely breathing. His designer shirt soaked, blood dried into the fabric. Salt crusted his lips. His eyes were shut, face swollen.

Rob rolled him over and Sanchez coughed violently—water, blood, and rage spilling out of his lungs like a demon being exorcised. He gasped, blinking wildly as life returned to his body. The last thing he remembered was his son… and Trayvon.

The betrayal burned hotter than the sun.

***

Two Weeks Later – Brooklyn

Trayvon stood in his private gym, towel around his neck, muscles glistening in sweat. He'd just finished a heavy set when his phone buzzed on the bench beside him. Unknown number. No name. Just one text.

"I'm alive."

His heart stopped for half a beat. Then the message continued.

"You should've finished the job… because now, I'm coming to finish you." – Sanchez

Trayvon stared at the screen, unmoving.

A single bead of sweat rolled down his cheek as the weight of his mistake crashed in.

Chapter 21

The thick steel door sealed out the world, locking in secrets that could bring down the most feared empire the city had ever known. The air was heavy, thick with cigarette smoke, stale coffee, Along the far wall, stretching nearly twenty feet, the IA task force's lifework stared back at them. A corkboard crammed with faces, crime scenes, names, phone numbers, bank statements, shell company and maps riddled with red string.

At the center of it all stood Lieutenant Marlena Greaves, her frame tense, her eyes like sharpened steel.

"This is it," she said, voice low but firm. "Everything we've been working for. Everything we've risked. It's all here. And now—now we show you how we know."

She tapped the board with the butt of her pen

It started quietly. A whisper of suspicion. A rumor that wouldn't die. But IA didn't move on gossip. They moved on proof.

Working in shadows alongside the feds, they secured court orders—sealed so tightly that not even the mayor's office caught wind. They planted bugs in cartel safehouses across Newark and the Bronx. They hacked burner phones that Porscha's crew thought were untouchable. They slipped trackers into unregistered vehicles, surveillance drones into the night sky, eyes and ears everywhere the criminals got comfortable.

They caught KP bragging about the hit on Boatwright over what he thought was a safe burner phone. "Clean work," he laughed. "Two in the skull, in and out. Bitch ain't see it coming."

Realz was worse, caught on a hidden camera unloading crates at a weapons drop. The footage was grainy, but his face was clear enough, and the audio left no doubt.

Most damning of all? The coded messages between Porscha and her lieutenants were decrypted. Plans for the murder of Detective Boatwright. The setup for Sammy the Don. The green light on Jessica. Every message tied Porscha to death after death.

***

Big Pete had flipped. That fat bastard, desperate to save his own skin, came crawling to IA months before he met his brutal end. In a cold interview room, sweating through his cheap suit, he spilled.

He gave names. Places. Timelines. He mapped Trayvon's operations down to where the bodies were burned or buried. He hinted at the truth behind Jessica's death—Trayvon's hand on the rope. And Pete even muttered about the yacht, about Escobar Sanchez's last moments. "His own son was setting him up," Pete had said, voice shaking. "Had Trayvon planning to do the dirty work. Like killin' a king for the crown."

And there was another CIA nameless soldier in the Lucchese family, one nobody saw coming. He fed IA details about the war with Pauly, about bodies dumped in places no one was supposed to find. "Buried where even your prayers can't reach," he'd whispered in a taped confession.

They found those graves. And IA added them to the board.

When the Bronx erupted in gunfire—Pauly's safehouse under siege—it wasn't just bodies IA collected. They found tech, encrypted phones, laptops with double-locked files.

It took weeks, but the tech team cracked them open. What spilled out was a goldmine. Messages confirming deals with Trayvon. Payment records to Porscha's shell companies. Photos of cash. Notes on planned hits. Routes for drug shipments from the docks. Pauly, Trayvon, Porscha—their alliance was in writing, in pictures, in files they thought could never be read.

***

The city's Financial Crimes Unit worked in silence, combing through records, chasing shadows. Offshore accounts in the Caymans. Shell companies in Panama. Fake charities, bogus consulting firms, silent partners who laundered millions. The paper trail led straight to Porscha and Trayvon.

Luxury cars paid for in cash. Mansions under dummy names. Art collections and diamonds, bought with cartel blood money. A web of lies meant to wash it clean—but IA untangled it strand by strand.

Surveillance Footage & License Plate Readers

Corey thought he was slick, speeding off on his motorcycle after murdering Boatwright. But a city traffic cam picked up his plates, caught his silhouette, clocked his speed as he fled the scene.

The Club Mercedes parking lot? A traffic cam aimed at the corner caught Lance's last moments alive—the flash of gunfire, the panicked faces in the background, the car rocking in the dark.

And Big Pete's murder? IA had footage of shadowy figures slipping away from the alley, a van ID'd leaving the scene minutes after the beating.

Piece by piece, the city itself became a witness.

***

Homeland Security had been on Escobar Sanchez for years. His double game, his secret talks with the government, his use of federal power to wipe out rivals—it was all buried in sealed files.

But Boatwright's death changed everything. The feds opened the books. They shared what they had. Sanchez's betrayals, his plans, his fall. And with that, IA understood why the bodies fell where they did. Why the wars started. Why Escobar's son wanted him dead.

They found the judge's body on the lake's edge, dumped like trash. Autopsy showed two shots to the head as the cause of death—he died before he hit the water.

Jessica's house told its own story. Blood on the floorboards. Marks on the beam where the rope had been tied. Trayvon's prints, faint but there.

Big Pete? DNA matched the weapons used on him. The blood splatter, the bruises, the broken bones—told of a savage beating, a message written in flesh.

Bullet casings matched Corey's gun. Prints, fibers, trace evidence—it was all there.

IA didn't rush. They watched. They listened. They waited. They let Porscha and Trayvon get comfortable, let them believe they were invisible. They let the web weave itself tight—until every thread led back to the spider.

And the city? The city bled in plain sight. Every murder another stain. Every betrayal another crack in the empire. Every cop or gangster who fell dragged another secret into the light. The Bronx massacre. The kidnapping of Flowers' children. Boatwright's execution. The club parking lot bloodbath. One by one, it added up.

Porscha underestimated them. She moved like a queen of ghosts—but even ghosts leave footprints. IA followed every single one.

The room was dead silent.

Lieutenant Greaves stepped back from the board. Her face was hard, her eyes wet with fury and exhaustion.

"This isn't luck," she said. Her voice was steady. "We know what we know because this team risked everything to pull the truth from hell itself. We bled for this. We burned friendships. We buried good cops. And now..."

She let the words hang, heavy as a noose.

"Now we're ready. Porscha Trayvon may think she owns this city. She may think she can hide behind her father, behind her money, behind her killers. But we're about to remind her. No one is untouchable.

The agents didn't cheer. They didn't clap. They just nodded—grim, ready.

Outside that sealed door, the city slept. But dawn was coming. And with it, the reckoning.

Chapter 22

It was a stormy night along the Jersey waterfront. Rain battered the windows of the abandoned warehouse, the kind of place where deals were made, lives ended, and secrets were buried. The stench of salt water, rust, and old oil filled the air. The Hudson River roared in the distance, waves crashing against forgotten docks.

Inside, the warehouse was dark, except for the dim glow of a single overhead light that flickered every so often, as if it was nervous about what was about to go down. The sound of boots echoed on the concrete floor as Mayor Rapkim paced slowly, his face drawn, eyes sunken with sleepless nights. He wasn't here as the polished politician tonight—he was here as a man trying to survive the firestorm that was closing in on all of them.

Across from him, Trayvon stood with his arms folded, jaw clenched, his eyes sharp but weary. The storm outside couldn't compare to the one raging in his mind. Porscha stood beside him, silent, cigar in hand, but her usual calm was gone. She felt it, the walls closing in, the pressure unlike anything she'd ever known.

And at the center of it all was FBI Senior Chief Henry Goldwyn, a man who didn't blink when staring death in the face. His suit was soaked at the shoulders from the rain, but he didn't care. He dropped a thick manila folder onto a rusted metal table between them. It hit the table with a sound that seemed to echo forever in that empty space.

"This," Goldwyn said, his voice cold, no trace of sympathy, "is your life. All of it. Every secret. Every body. Every deal. Every betrayal. And this—" he tapped the folder with two fingers, "—is what's about to bury you both. Unless we can try and stop it and that's not guaranteed."

Porscha flicked her cigar away, the ember hissing as it hit a puddle. She didn't say a word. Her eyes locked on that folder like it was a loaded gun aimed at her head.

Mayor Rapkim exhaled hard, running a hand over his face. "I didn't want it to come to this. God knows I didn't. But IA... they're coming. And this time, it ain't just some rookie cops and detectives looking for a payday. They got the feds. They got Homeland. They got the goddamn Attorney General breathing down their necks. And they got names. Witnesses. Evidence."

Trayvon's voice was low, deadly calm. "Who?"

Goldwyn smiled, but it was a dead man's smile. "You want the list? Fine. Let's start with the easy ones. Big Pete. That rat's been feeding them for months. You didn't think he died because he was shot, did you? He was in protective custody. He gave them everything. Maps. Drops. Contacts. Murders me."

Trayvon's fists clenched so hard his knuckles went white.

Goldwyn continued, flipping the folder open, spreading photos across the table. Crime scenes. Bodies. Wiretap transcripts. Surveillance shots of Porscha, Trayvon, their crew. "Pauly's people? Yeah, a few of them flipped after Lucchese's bloodbath in the Bronx. They're singing like goddamn canaries. And don't think for one second your friend Escobar Sanchez is safe. His own attorney Mr. Wright gave them what we needed to tie him to half the murders on the East Coast. Homeland's already moving on him. The New York Commission? Broken. The Italians? Eating each other alive. And through all that chaos, you two? You're the centerpiece."

Porscha finally found her voice. It came out hoarse. "What are you saying?"

"I'm saying this is bigger than your little empire," Mayor Rapkim said, stepping forward, his tone almost pleading. "I've tried to shield you. Christ, I've done things that would make the devil blush to keep the heat off. But this? This is the end game. You're looking at the death penalty, Porscha. Both of you. This ain't just about drugs anymore. Or guns. Or even the bodies. They're calling you domestic terrorists. They want to make an example of you."

Porscha's heart pounded in her chest. Death penalty. The words echoed in her mind like gunshots. She'd always thought she could outsmart, outfight, outlast. But this? This was a noose tightening around her neck.

Trayvon's voice was ice. "Who else is cooperating?"

Goldwyn started laying it out, one by one, like daggers to the heart.

"Pauly's sister, she telling everything. She knows that Lucchese had her son killed. Yeah. She talking. She spilling the beans. She's under protection. She's been spilling everything about Lucchese, and about your connections she knows about, Trayvon."

"Flowers? His kids being taken was the last straw. He's working with them now. He wants justice. He's naming names everything over the last two years he knows."

"Boatwright's death? They know how that went down. The funeral hit. The shooter. They got witnesses. They got the bike. They got ballistics. Porscha, they're going to hang that one on you personally."

"Jessica? You thought nobody knew? Trayvon, you didn't even cover your tracks, cameras you didn't know were there, DNA from the scene your sweat. Slam dunk."

Goldwyn leaned in, his eyes hard as steel. "And then there's the judge. The lake. The body. You thought dumping him on shore was smart? They got the trace evidence from your car tires, Trayvon. All of it. From the store you stopped by when you left. You're on camera."

Porscha felt the room spin. For the first time, she felt fear—not the kind she'd felt in gunfights or standoffs, but deep, soul-crushing fear. She was trapped. Every angle covered. Every move anticipated.

Rapkim's voice softened. "There's only one way out of this and it's not a way out." Mayor Rapkim swallowed hard. "I have a friend who give me all of this information yesterday, me and Henry. I'm standing here telling you there's no more favors after this one. No more shields. This is it. We all had a good run but it's over, this is the last stand. Blow the building up with everyone inside, all the evidence is up in smoke and just pray there's no hard drive nowhere else. Now out of ten times, this is so top secret there's not, but it's always that one percent chance."

Goldwyn folded his arms. "You got two choices. Run, and die tired. Or sit down, and maybe—maybe—we can negotiate life without parole instead of lethal injection, or your third option... do what the mayor say, blow the fucking building to smoke."

The rain pounded harder outside. Thunder rolled like the heavens themselves were passing judgment.

Porscha swallowed hard. She looked at Trayvon. The man she'd idolized. The man she'd followed into this dark world. His eyes met hers. For the first time, there was no plan in them. No way out. Just grim acceptance.

"You knew this day would come," Trayvon said quietly.

Porscha nodded. "I just didn't think it'd be today."

Goldwyn gave them a moment before speaking again. "You think about your crew. You think about who's left standing. Because they're next. They are coming for all of them. Realz. Corey. Paris. Everyone. And when they're done, your entire organization? Gone. Like it never existed."

Porscha took a deep breath. Her voice was steady, but inside she was falling apart. "Give us the building location.

This is the last move on the chess board and I'm going to make it?"

Goldwyn smiled that dead smile again. "Names. Evidence. Everything up in smoke. I knew you was going to say that. Porscha, everything will be in your hands tomorrow before noon you have a window of seventy-two hours. After this, take your crew and disappear for a few weeks or months until you hear from me."

The silence that followed was deafening.

"No! We not going nowhere. I worked too hard to leave what I have behind. I want the names and addresses of the rats. If I die in the streets so be it, but they are going to die period." Henry just nodded, he respected Porscha. She wasn't like the rest, she was a real killer and businesswoman who stood on that.

Outside, the storm raged on. But inside that warehouse, it felt like the storm had already hit—and left nothing but ruins.

Chapter 23

The night air was heavy, suffocating in its stillness. Porscha stood alone under the pale glow of the moon, the cold steel of her pistol in one hand, the slow burn of her cigar in the other. The time for mercy had long passed. She knew what had to be done—and this time, she wasn't going to flinch. Not for KP. Not for anyone.

KP had been loyal once. But loyalty was as fragile as glass in this game, and his shattered the moment he opened his mouth on a wiretapped phone. Porscha had warned them all. No phones. No loose talk. And yet here they were, the feds closing in because KP couldn't keep his trap shut about Boatwright's hit. Porscha's heart was ice as she approached the secluded winery on the outskirts of the city, their meeting spot.

Inside, the room fell silent as she entered. The air was thick with the stench of old oak barrels, wine, and fear. KP stood near the head of the table, trying to mask his guilt. But Porscha saw it plain as day. She flicked her cigar ash on the floor and locked eyes on him.

"You was running your fucking mouth off over the phone," she spat, her voice low, deadly. "About the hit on Detective Boatwright. The FBI got it all on tape. All of it."

KP's eyes went wide, lips parting to offer some desperate excuse, but Porscha didn't give him the chance. In one fluid motion, the gun rose, a deafening crack split the room, and KP hit the floor with a bullet through his skull—gone before his body even realized it. Blood pooled beneath him, a stark reminder of what betrayal cost.

No one moved. No one spoke. They stared at Porscha like she was death itself. And maybe she was.

"This meeting ain't over," she said coldly, holstering the weapon. "Now listen…"

The sharp scent of cigar smoke hung heavy in the air of the dimly lit winery's backroom. The clink of glasses and murmurs of uneasy voices punctuated the tense silence. Porscha stood at the center, cool and commanding, her dark eyes flashing with a ruthless fire that burned hotter than the cigar clenched between her lips.

Around her, the faces of her trusted lieutenants—Paris, Corey, and Rakim—were masked in shadows, their expressions unreadable but taut with anticipation. This was no ordinary meeting. Tonight, everything would change. The stakes were higher than ever, and the threat of exposure loomed over them like a guillotine's blade.

Porscha crushed the stub of her cigar into an ashtray, her gaze sweeping the room. "KP was talkin' too much," she said coldly. "You all know what happened to him. That shit can't happen again. We're cleaning house."

The room swallowed her words. They all witnessed KP's murder. Shot in cold blood by Porscha herself, not just to send a message, but to silence him forever. The FBI had been closing in, and KP's careless mouth had almost sealed their fate.

She stepped forward, pulling out a crumpled sheet of paper. "This is where it's all happening. My case file, the evidence, the dirt on us—all stored inside that building." She nodded sharply toward the address she'd written down, eyes gleaming with cold purpose. "That place has to go up in smoke."

A murmur ran through the room.

Paris, ever the loyal shadow, slipped forward, a heavy suitcase in hand. She moved with practiced stealth, the disguise she wore obscuring her features—nondescript clothes, a cheap wig, gloves to mask her fingerprints. No one could tell it was her beneath the layers.

Rakim and Corey were just the same, each carrying identical-looking suitcases, their disguises flawless and grim.

Porscha's voice was steady, unyielding. "Inside each of those cases are three blocks of C4—enough to level two city blocks if we wanted. But we only need to make sure this building burns down to nothing. No evidence, no witnesses. We're going dark."

She watched as Paris disappeared into the bathroom. Quietly, she set the suitcase down behind the stall door, hidden from plain sight but ready to be triggered.

Rakim and Corey did the same, slipping their deadly cargo into strategic corners of the building. The plan was simple and brutal, blow the evidence—and anyone left inside—to hell.

Porscha took a long drag on her cigar, her thoughts wandering to the consequences. "This ain't just a cleanup. This is war. The feds, Internal Affairs—they wanna see us rot behind bars, or worse. We give 'em nothing but ashes."

The room fell silent again, the weight of her words sinking in.

***

Outside the building, the world was oblivious. But inside, tension crackled like static electricity. Everyone except Lieutenant Marlena Greaves was inside the building. Porscha had made sure of that. Greaves, the relentless IA investigator, was known for her dogged pursuit of truth. But tonight, even her meticulous planning wouldn't save her.

The explosion ripped through the building like a violent thunderclap, the concussive force so fierce it shattered windows blocks away. The night sky was suddenly lit by an inferno swallowing the entire structure, smoke billowing high and dark.

Porscha stepped back, crushing the last of her cigar beneath her heel, watching the chaos with a cold, calculating smile.

"There's a special place for me in hell," she whispered, "but hell's got nothing on me."

Earlier that evening, Porscha had summoned her closest allies for an urgent gathering at the winery. The air was thick with tension, the kind that only comes before irrevocable decisions are made.

KP's death still hung in the room like a ghost. No one spoke his name, but his absence was a silent warning.

Paris sat near Porscha, her expression unreadable, but her hands trembled ever so slightly as she adjusted the strap on her bag.

Corey leaned against the wall, arms crossed, jaw clenched tight.

Rakim paced near the entrance, eyes darting to every corner, every shadow.

Porscha's voice cut through the room, sharp and commanding. "We've been compromised. The feds got a wiretap on KP, heard his mouth runnin' off 'bout Boatwright's hit. Before he could even blink, I put a bullet in his head."

A silence fell. The others nodded grimly.

"This meeting ain't just to talk. It's to execute."

Her gaze swept over them, reading every flicker of doubt or fear.

"I got the address where they're holdin' all the evidence—the damning shit on us. It's the heart of this whole mess."

She slammed the paper down on the table. "We're takin' it out tonight. No traces left. No witnesses. No loose ends."

Paris spoke up, voice low but steady. "Are you sure about this, Porscha? This kind of fire will light the whole city up. There's no turning back."

Porscha nodded. "I'm sure. We don't just survive this. We crush it."

Corey broke into a bitter grin. "Blow it all to hell. I like the sound of that."

Rakim stopped pacing and faced them. "Timing's key. We get in, plant the explosives, and get out before anyone even knows what hit 'em."

Porscha pulled three identical black suitcases from behind the bar, each heavy with a deadly secret. "Each of these holds three blocks of C4. Enough to level this whole building, and then some."

She handed one to Paris, who slipped it behind her disguise, nearly invisible.

"One block's enough to take down two floors. But I'm packing enough to make sure there's no evidence left at all."

The room grew colder, the weight of what they were about to do settling on everyone's shoulders.

***

The old government evidence building was nondescript — a plain brick box tucked away in a designated federal zone. It was secure, supposedly impenetrable, but tonight it would be a tomb.

Paris moved with silent grace, her heart pounding as she navigated the dimly lit hallways.

She found the bathroom and slipped inside, the heavy suitcase thudding softly as she set it down behind the stall door.

Corey and Rakim were doing the same, placing their deadly cargo in key locations near evidence lockers, data servers, and filing rooms.

They had a narrow window to get out and detonate remotely, making sure no one was left to interfere.

Porscha waited in the winery, her phone in hand, ready to trigger the blast.

Every detail had been planned with ruthless precision.

The explosion was deafening, the blast shaking the earth and lighting the sky with flames. Sirens wailed in the distance as the building became a blazing inferno.

But inside, no one moved. No one escaped.

Porscha leaned back in her chair, exhaling smoke from her cigar, the glow of the fire reflecting in her eyes.

She whispered, "This is just the beginning. They wanted war? They got it."

Her loyalty was clear, no one — not even the people closest to her — would stand in the way of protecting her and her father.

The ruthless queen of this empire had just made sure the threat was gone. Permanently.

Chapter 24

The night sky was no longer dark over that desolate stretch of city street. Where a fortified federal complex once stood—a place where secrets were kept, cases built, and justice forged—there was now only fire. An inferno. A smoldering ruin of smoke, twisted steel, and ash.

The acrid scent of burning concrete and scorched files choked the air for blocks. Even seasoned first responders staggered under the weight of it, their faces streaked with sweat and soot as they fought against an enemy that could no longer be saved.

The sirens never stopped. Their wail echoed through the night, mingling with the low rumble of the fire and the stunned sobs of those who watched their city's heart burn.

Angela Dorsey stood at the edge of the barricade, the heat of the blaze hot against her face. As a veteran reporter, she had seen crime scenes, disasters, tragedy—but nothing like this. Nothing that felt so final, so cruel.

What was once the nerve center of justice is now an open grave, she thought as she clutched her notepad with trembling fingers. "We're not just witnessing the destruction of a building tonight. We're witnessing the murder of truth."

Beyond the barricade, the building groaned as its structure failed, sending sparks and debris into the night.

And then came Lieutenant Marlena Greaves.

Through the chaos of flashing lights and rising smoke, she arrived—her car screeching to a stop, door flung open, boots hitting pavement like gunshots. Her hair was

147

disheveled, jacket thrown hastily over a t-shirt, badge swinging wildly from her neck as she pushed through the cordon.

She didn't see the cameras. She didn't hear the reporters calling her name.

Her eyes were locked on the destruction.

She walked forward as if in a daze, like someone caught in the worst kind of dream—the kind you can't wake up from.

Angela watched her, heart breaking at the sight.

Lieutenant Greaves stopped at the edge of the barricade. The fire's heat blasted her, but she didn't move. She just stared at the inferno that had, moments before, been everything she and her team had fought to build.

A year of work. Hundreds of lives touched by those files, that evidence.

And now—gone.

She spoke, not to the cameras, not even to Angela, but to herself. A whisper lost in the roar of flames.

"A year... A year of work. Gone. Just like that."

Angela stepped closer. She had to ask, even though she already knew the answer. "Who would do this?"

Lieutenant Greaves didn't look at her. Her voice was low. Bitter.

"We both know the answer to that. This wasn't random. This wasn't an accident. This was murder. Of my team. Of justice. And whoever did this... they've just declared war."

Names began to filter through the smoke, carried on the grief-stricken voices of survivors and first responders.

Derek Langston. Thirty-four. Father of two. Last seen poring over wiretap transcripts that might have cracked the case wide open.

Susan Wells. Fifty-one. Thirty years in the justice system. Known for baking birthday cakes for everyone in the office.

Jamie Chen. Twenty-seven. Bright. Engaged to be married. A future stolen in fire and fury.

Greaves heard the names and closed her eyes, as if trying to block out the pain. But it was no use. These were her people.

"They were family," she said, voice shaking. "People think of us as cold. Hard. But we bleed. We love. And tonight, we lost family."

Her hands balled into fists.

"I promised their families they'd come home safe. I promised them we'd bring the bad guys down. And now… now I have to make new promises. That I'll find who did this. That they won't rest. Not for a second."

Angela turned her gaze to the fire crews, working with desperate fury against an enemy that already won. Captain Rios wiped soot from his eyes, his voice raw.

"We're doing everything we can. But it's… it's bad. The heat was so intense, the building went up like tinder. Whoever did this—this was no accident. They wanted to erase that place. And they've succeeded."

His voice broke. "I knew people in there. Good people. This is a tragedy."

Everywhere Angela looked, she saw the same stunned faces. Some firefighters wept openly. Some officers clung to one another for strength. And beyond them, citizens gathered—some holding candles, some holding each other, all united by shock and sorrow.

Statements from the mayor's office were swift. "An unspeakable act of terrorism against justice itself," the mayor said.

Vigils began to take shape even as the fire still burned. The community reeled, unable to comprehend the scale of what had been lost.

Dawn crept over the horizon, bathing the smoking ruin in pale light.

Greaves hadn't moved. She stood sentinel over the ashes, eyes burning with a fury that would not be extinguished.

Angela found the courage to ask one last question. "What comes next?"

Greaves turned, and in that moment, she didn't look broken. She looked dangerous.

"I don't care what it takes," she said, voice like steel. "I don't care who I have to go through. I will find them. And they will pay."

Her gaze drifted back to the wreckage.

"I owe them that much."

The city mourned that day. And somewhere, in the shadows, the monsters who set the fire watched it burn, knowing they had lit a fuse that could never be snuffed out.

Chapter 25

The air in Mayor Rapkim's private office was thick with tension, heavier than the smoke still rising over the city. The skyline was bruised, an ugly smear of fire and ash where the federal building had once stood. The city that never slept now felt like it couldn't breathe.

Rapkim stood at the window, hands clasped behind his back, staring out into that wounded night. His tie hung loose, shirt sleeves rolled up, sweat dampening the fabric at his neck. He didn't turn when the door opened. He already knew who it was, he was expecting him

Henry Goldwyn stepped in quietly, closing the door behind him with a soft click. The senior director of the FBI looked as exhausted as the mayor felt. His suit jacket was gone, his usually neat hair disheveled, eyes dark from hours without rest. Mayor Rapkim had already written down on a piece of paper, "There are bugs in my office. IA is watching me. Word got back to me after the explosion within ten hours before I got to my office, it was already known. We're going to play this off as if we don't know nothing to cover our asses."

Senior Director Goldwyn read the letter and nodded. He'd already gotten word that IA was watching everyone, so he was coming to inform the mayor, if he didn't know. So, he played the role with the mayor, knowing this was their dirty work and Porscha just covered all their asses. He winked at the mayor and set the note on fire and placed it in the ashtray.

Neither man spoke at first. There was too much to say, and no words felt big enough, but they had to play this off. They had to make the conversation believable.

Finally, Rapkim broke the silence.

"You see that out there, Henry?" His voice was low, like he was afraid the city itself might overhear. "That... that's our legacy going up in smoke."

Goldwyn exhaled slowly, his voice heavy. "I see it. And I smell it. And I feel it in my goddamn bones."

Rapkim turned then, his face pale and drawn, his eyes hollow. "How? How did she pull this off? We had safeguards. Layers of them. That building was a fortress."

Goldwyn shook his head, rubbing a hand down his face. "It was a fortress, until it wasn't. Porscha didn't just hit us tonight, Mayor. She gutted us. And she did it clean. Efficient. No loose ends. That was military-level precision."

Rapkim sank into the leather chair behind his desk, the weight of the night crashing down on him. "We underestimated her. All of us. We thought she was just some... some thug's daughter playing queen in daddy's empire."

Goldwyn leaned on the edge of the desk, his voice dropping to a near whisper. "She's not playin'. Porscha is the real thing. A boss in her own right. And what scares me the most? She's cold enough to kill everyone in that building—people she didn't even know—just to protect herself and that bastard father of hers."

Rapkim stared at him, disbelief and grudging respect mixing in his gaze. "You're telling me we're up against a woman who just handed us one of the worst domestic attacks this city has ever seen... and she'll sleep like a baby tonight?"

Goldwyn didn't hesitate. "Damn right I am."

The mayor let out a bitter laugh, no humor in it. "And we had her in our sights. We had her, Henry! All that evidence... gone. Just like that."

Goldwyn nodded grimly. "She knew exactly where the files were. Where the recordings were stored. Where the bodies were buried, figuratively and literally. And she wiped it all out in under an hour."

A long silence stretched between them, broken only by the faint sirens in the distance.

"We need to get ahead of this," Rapkim said finally. "The press, the public—they'll want answers. They'll want heads on spikes."

"They'll get them," Goldwyn promised. "But we need to be smart. Porscha made her move. Now it's our turn. No more underestimating her. No more thinking of her as some cartel princess. She's the goddamn queen now."

Rapkim's eyes narrowed. "You're scared of her."

Goldwyn straightened, meeting his gaze. "I'm scared of what she's willing to do. We've dealt with cartels before, mayor. We've dealt with mafia dons, drug kings, domestic terrorists. But this? This is something else. Porscha doesn't just want to survive. She wants to erase anyone who threatens her. She plays chess while the rest of us are playing checkers. And tonight… she just took out our queen and half the board in one move."

Rapkim drummed his fingers on the desk, thinking. "So, what's the play? How do we stop her?"

Goldwyn's face was hard, his voice deadly quiet. "We stop playing by the rules. That's the only way to beat someone like Porscha. We use every tool we've got. We burn her network down, piece by piece. No more waiting for warrants. No more red tape. We go to war."

The mayor's jaw tightened. "War. Against a woman who just made the FBI look like fools."

"She didn't just make us look like fools," Goldwyn said. "She made us look weak. And if we don't answer that, loud and fast, every other crew in this country will start making moves."

Rapkim stood, going to the window again. The city was starting to stir, the first rays of sun slicing through the smoke.

"She's not done," he said quietly. "You know that, right? This wasn't the end game. This was just the opening shot."

Goldwyn nodded. "I know."

"And Henry…"

"Yeah?"

Rapkim turned, his face set. "Don't miss. We don't get another shot at her." Both men smiled at each other, knowing they just made their story believable.

***

Don Lucchese sat in his study, a heavy crystal glass of bourbon untouched in his hand. Across from him, Nick the Boss leaned forward, elbows on his knees, eyes dark with worry.

"Porscha," Lucchese said at last, the name tasting like ash on his tongue. "That girl… that woman… she just sent the whole city a message. And we'd be fools not to hear it loud and clear."

Nick nodded, running a hand through his hair. "She ain't playin' around. That wasn't just some cartel hit. That was art. Bloody, brutal art."

Lucchese's lips twitched into something like a smile—a smile without warmth. "You always said she had steel in her. But this? This was something else. She took out a federal building. Evidence, agents, cops… all in one move. No hesitation. No mercy."

"She's got bigger balls than half the guys in this game," Nick muttered. "I'm tellin' you, boss. Porscha ain't just a cartel princess no more. She's the queen. The real thing."

Lucchese sipped his bourbon finally, letting the burn remind him he was alive. "And now what? We do what? Sit back and let her run this city?"

Nick shook his head. "Nah. We can't just let it go. But we gotta be smart. Porscha's got respect now. From everyone. After tonight, even the old heads in Miami, Chicago, L.A.? They'll be watching her. And they'll be thinking twice before crossing her."

Lucchese stared into the fire, the flames reflecting in his eyes. "She made herself untouchable. That's what she did. And I'll tell you this, Nicky—I don't like it. Not one bit."

Nick leaned closer, voice low. "So, what's the move?"

Lucchese didn't answer right away. He watched the fire, thinking, the gears turning behind his cold gaze.

"We don't move on her. Not yet. Let the feds bleed themselves dry trying. Let the city tear itself apart. And when Porscha makes a mistake—and she will—then we strike."

Nick sat back, blowing out a slow breath. "You're playin' the long game."

Lucchese smiled, a predator's smile. "Always. And Porscha? She might be queen today. But the thing about queens, Nicky... they all fall eventually."

Chapter 26

Detective Flowers had one thing on his mind, get out of town before it was too late. He let IA investigator Lieutenant Greaves talk him into going against Porscha, knowing how deadly she is. Greaves's swore to protect him and his children if he'd just help her get Porscha. She needed him to work on the case with her. It was a mistake he wished he could take back now, but it was too late. He had to get out of New York. He was making this move nobody knew anything about. His heart pounded so hard he feared it might give him away as he was trying to sneak out of the city. Detective Flowers had always believed in justice. He'd spent his life chasing it, hunting criminals, protecting the innocent. But tonight, justice felt far away, slipping through his fingers like smoke.

His boots echoed softly on the cracked pavement as he moved through the dimly lit streets of the city. Every nerve in his body screamed for him to keep moving, to vanish into the shadows. He wasn't just running from the law—he was running from death.

The Investigation Building had been his base for months. The heart of the operation to take down the cartel that had poisoned their city for years. Now, that heart was burning.

The explosion had been deafening. The ground had trembled beneath him. Flames clawed their way up the building's side, casting dancing shadows that flickered like ghosts.

Flowers' breath came in ragged gasps as he stumbled backward, eyes fixed on the inferno. He felt a crushing weight in his chest, a mix of dread, fear, and the bitter sting of defeat. All he saw was two black SUVs coming his way His instincts screamed. He was surrounded.

Masked figures materialized from the darkness—fast, coordinated, merciless.

Detective Flowers raised his fists, every strike powered by desperation. But Rakim was relentless—his fist connected with a brutal force that sent Elijah crashing down.

Pinned beneath a swarm of bodies, his breath shallow and his vision blurred, Detective Flowers caught a glimpse of Porscha stepping out of the shadows.

She was ice incarnate—serene, deadly.

And then he saw his children, their innocent eyes wide with terror.

"Please," Detective Flowers begged, voice breaking. "Don't."

Porscha didn't hesitate.

Gunshots echoed.

Silence.

Elijah's world shattered.

Porscha's footsteps were soft but carried the weight of inevitability. The children, clutching each other, were the last pieces of Detective Flowers' heart. Their screams were swallowed by the night.

She raised the gun, steady as death itself.

"Don't!" Detective Flowers' voice cracked, raw with pain and disbelief. "No, please!"

Her finger squeezed the trigger.

The shots shattered the silence like thunderclaps.

The children fell, motionless.

Detective Flowers screamed—a sound filled with agony, rage, and loss.

Porscha looked at him once, the faintest hint of something unspoken in her eyes, before turning away.

Rakim's gun rose, fired, and Detective Flowers' life ended in a single, brutal moment.

The black SUV disappeared into the night, tires screeching softly against the pavement.

A haunting stillness lingered over the scene.

Detective Flowers was gone.

His children—gone.

And the city was left to drown in the cold silence of loss.

***

The night was thick with tension, the kind that seemed to press down on the city like a storm that refused to break. The moon hung low and heavy, casting an eerie silver sheen over the quiet, forgotten streets of an industrial yard on the outskirts of town. The hum of distant freight trains was the only sound, the world holding its breath for what was about to unfold.

Trayvon stood with his back to a battered warehouse wall, his hands in his coat pockets, his eyes sharp beneath the brim of his hat. His face was carved from stone, with the weight of power and responsibility etched into every line. This wasn't just another meeting. This was history.

The headlights of a black Bentley crept through the darkness, the engine purring like a predator that knew no fear. The car stopped a few feet from Trayvon, and after a long pause, the driver's door opened.

Don Lucchese stepped out. No guards. No entourage. Just a man who needed none. His tailored coat flowed behind him as he approached, his eyes locked with Trayvon's. Two worlds meeting in the dead of night. Mafia and cartel. Blood and empire.

For a moment, neither spoke. They simply studied each other—the way warriors once did on the eve of battle. Respect was instant. Both men saw it in the other's posture, the calm that only came from standing over graves you dug yourself, the knowledge that in this world, kings were self-made or dead.

Lucchese broke the silence first, his voice low, steady.

"Trayvon."

Trayvon nodded once. "Lucchese."

They shook hands, firm and slow, like sealing an unspoken pact.

"I heard a lot about you over the years," Lucchese said, his gaze unwavering.

"I could say the same," Trayvon replied. "But I don't deal in rumors. I wanted to see the man for myself."

Lucchese smirked faintly. "And?"

"You're everything they say you are. And more."

Lucchese's smirk faded into something harder. "You don't call a meeting like this for pleasantries. Tell me what I need to know."

Trayvon took a breath, his eyes scanning the shadows before returning to Lucchese's face. "There was a meeting. A critical one. Porscha called it. She's handling business that needed to be handled. I won't tell you who else was there. Doesn't matter. Only name that matters is hers. The point is... the building where that meeting was being watched. Listened to. Recorded."

Lucchese's eyes narrowed, face expressionless, but Trayvon could feel the fire burning behind them.

"The feds? IA?" Lucchese asked.

Trayvon nodded. "Both. Pauly's sister... she's the source. She's been working with them behind everyone's back. Feeding them piece after piece. That's why the building had to go. There was no choice."

Lucchese absorbed that, his face a mask of steel.

"But that's not the end of it," Trayvon continued. "She's still talking to them. Still giving them whatever they want. And she won't stop. You know what that means."

Lucchese didn't answer right away. He stared into the night, the weight of what had to be done settling on him like an old coat. When he spoke, his voice was like ice cutting through the dark.

"We're all players on this chessboard, Trayvon. I see that now. Every piece has a role. And if one piece betrays the game… it has to be removed. I'll take care of it. Myself."

Trayvon inclined his head. "I knew you'd understand. That's why I came to you."

Without another word, Lucchese turned and got back in his car. The engine roared to life, and with a flick of his headlights, he disappeared into the night.

***

Lucchese didn't go back to his mansion. He didn't call his men. This was personal. Pauly's sister, Annette, had been a thorn festering too long. He thought by having her son killed. she would know to watch where she stepped. That was her and Pauly's problem. His biggest mistake was he had trusted her loyalty by proxy, trusted that blood meant something. But in the end, blood meant nothing without honor, that's why he did what he did.

It wasn't hard to find her. She thought she was clever, bouncing from motel to motel on the edge of town, but Lucchese's network was a net too tight to slip through. By midnight, he was standing outside a run-down roadside inn, the neon sign flickering weakly.

He entered the lobby, paid cash, and walked the stairs in silence, his steps soft as death itself. The hallway smelled of old smoke and rot. He stopped at the door—room 12. He could hear her inside, pacing, talking on the phone in hushed, frantic tones.

"…I don't care what he said, I want protection. I gave you everything—names, locations, deals. I want. You promised me I'd be safe. No, no, don't hang up—"

Lucchese knocked, once.

Silence.

Then, "Who is it?"

Lucchese didn't answer.

A pause. The sound of a chain sliding into place, then the door cracked open an inch. Annette's frightened eyes appeared through the gap.

That was the last thing she saw.

Lucchese kicked the door open with brutal force, the chain snapping, sending her sprawling backward. The phone clattered to the floor. Before she could scream, he was on her, his gloved hand clamped over her mouth, his other hand around her throat.

She thrashed, but he was too strong, too controlled. He dragged her into the room, kicked the door shut behind him. Her eyes bulged with terror as he stared down at her, the calm of a man delivering justice long overdue.

"You chose this," Lucchese said softly. "You could have stayed loyal. You could have kept your mouth shut. But you chose this."

She tried to shake her head, tried to plead, but he didn't care for her words. Words were lies.

Lucchese pulled a slender blade from inside his coat, the edge honed to a deadly gleam. Without hesitation, he slid it between her teeth, slicing downward in one smooth, horrifying motion. The blade ripped through her tongue, severing it, the blood gushing hot and fast. Her screams were a wet gurgling horror.

He let her fall to the floor, gasping, choking on her own blood. He watched as she writhed, the betrayal leaving her body along with her life.

Lucchese knelt beside her, his voice soft as he wiped the blade clean.

"No more talking, Annette. No more lies. No more betrayal."

She stilled, the life leaving her eyes as the red pool spread beneath her.

Lucchese rose, calm as ever, and walked to the window. He stared out at the quiet night, the stars cold and distant.

One piece removed. The game continued.

***

By dawn, Lucchese stood on the balcony of his home, watching the city wake beneath him. The call came—Trayvon's voice on the other end.

"It's done," Lucchese said simply.

Trayvon didn't ask how. He didn't need to.

"Respect, Lucchese. We're going to win this game."

Lucchese nodded to himself. "We are. And when we do…we'll reshape this city in our image."

Trayvon chuckled darkly. "Damn right."

The call ended, the alliance sealed in blood.

The city was theirs now—a chessboard where the kings moved in the shadows, unseen but all-powerful. The feds would keep looking. IA would keep digging. But the players who mattered knew the truth, there was no room for betrayal in this game. Only victory. Or death.

Lucchese lit a cigar, inhaled deeply, and let the smoke curl into the morning air. He thought of Annette's eyes as the life fled them. He thought of the blade, of the silence that followed.

Justice wasn't clean. It wasn't pretty. But it was necessary.

And the kings of this world understood that better than anyone.

Chapter 27

The jungle was a beast all its own—alive, watching, waiting to consume anyone who dared cross Escobar Sanchez.

No one knew where the true boss of the Sanchez Cartel made his home.

Escobar Sanchez stood at the edge of his balcony, the humid night air clinging to his skin like a second shirt. The jungle stretched before him, black and endless, the perfect graveyard for traitors.

His mind wasn't on the stars.

It was on blood.

His own son's blood.

Escobar clenched the railing so hard his knuckles turned white. The boy he'd raised, protected, taught the rules of the game—that boy had tried to end him. On the yacht. In front of God. In front of men.

And now? That boy—that snake—was marked.

Escobar's voice, when it came, was soft. Deadly soft.

"Dead or alive. I don't care which. Bring me my son's head. And burn anyone who stands beside him."

Behind him, Toro, his most loyal enforcer, nodded.

"It will be done, Patrón. The jungle will drink deep tonight."

An SUV crunched its way up the gravel path leading to the compound. Inside, Mr. Wright— the cartel's lawyer, the man who once held Escobar's secrets in the palm of his hand—dabbed sweat from his brow with a silk handkerchief.

He didn't like being called out here. Not at night. Not alone.

"This place…" he muttered to himself, glancing at the high walls, the watchtowers, the floodlights. It felt less like a home and more like a prison.

Armed men met him at the gate, machetes at their sides, faces blank as stone. They said nothing as they escorted him inside.

Mr. Wright tried to steady his nerves.

You've done nothing wrong.

You've always been loyal.

But the knot in his gut told a different story.

Escobar waited inside the room they called La Sala Roja—the red room.

It was bare. A steel table. Two chairs. A single swinging bulb that cast more shadow than light. A drain in the center of the floor. A bucket in the corner.

Escobar sat in silence, his blade resting on the table like a sleeping serpent.

When Mr. Wright entered, his smile was forced, tight at the corners.

"Escobar," he greeted, voice too loud in the stillness. "I wasn't expecting this meeting. Everything all right?"

Escobar motioned to the chair.

"Sit."

Mr. Wright obeyed.

For a long moment, they sat in silence. The jungle's night chorus filled the space between them.

Finally, Escobar spoke.

"Tell me… when did you decide to betray me?"

The words hit like a hammer. Mr. Wright's breath hitched.

"I—I don't know what you mean. Escobar, I would never—"

Escobar's gaze darkened.

"You gave Internal Affairs everything. My accounts. My partners. My routes. My son's locations. You spoke to them like a woman in confession. Did you think I wouldn't know?"

Mr. Wright's face turned to ash. His tongue felt thick in his mouth.

"Please, Escobar—listen to me. They came for me. They had leverage. My wife. My son. I had no choice. But I fed them lies. I swear it. I protected you!"

Escobar rose slowly. The chair scraped against the floor.

"No choice?" His voice was a whisper now, dangerous and low. "A man always has a choice. And you chose yourself over me."

Two guards stepped from the shadows, seizing Mr. Wright by the arms, dragging him to his knees.

"Escobar! Please! We can fix this! I'm loyal!"

Escobar's blade glinted under the swaying bulb.

"No. A loyal man dies before he speaks.

Escobar knelt in front of him, his face inches away, breath like smoke.

"Your words cost me. Your words almost cost me my life. So, let's take them first."

From his coat he drew iron tongs, cold and heavy. He pried Mr. Wright's mouth open despite the man's frantic struggle.

The blade sliced.

Mr. Wright's tongue hit the floor with a wet slap. Blood flooded his mouth. His scream was a wet gurgle.

Escobar stood, watching as his once-trusted lawyer writhed, choking on his own betrayal.

"String him up outside the gates. Let the jungle decide what's left of him."

The guards dragged him out, his blood leaving a trail behind.

By dawn, Mr. Wright's body hung from a tree outside the compound, his tongue stuffed in his pocket, his lifeless eyes staring at nothing. Vultures circled above, waiting.

The men who saw him would speak of it in hushed tones for generations, the fate of those who crossed Escobar Sanchez.

Inside the compound, Escobar poured himself a glass of rum, his hands steady. Toro stood at his side, waiting for orders.

"Burn the accounts. Move the money. Tonight."

"And the son, Patrón?"

Escobar's eyes burned like coals.

"Wanted. Dead or alive. Bring me his head. And any fool who stands beside him. No mercy. No deals."

Toro nodded.

"The jungle will drink deep, Patrón."

Escobar raised his glass.

"To loyalty."

And somewhere, deep in the jungle, the hunt began.

***

The cold, sterile air of the morgue clung to Lieutenant Marlena Greaves like a suffocating shroud as she exited the building. The echo of her boots on the polished floor seemed deafening in the silence that followed her. She paused at the exit, gripping the steel doorframe with trembling fingers, trying to steady herself. But no amount of deep breathing could calm the storm raging inside her. Her chest felt tight, her throat raw, her eyes stung from the tears she refused to let fall.

But they fell anyway.

Marlena had stared at the bodies of Detective Flowers and his children for what felt like hours. The lifeless forms of those two little ones—innocent, pure, full of promise—lay on the cold slabs, their faces pale, their eyes closed forever. And Flowers… her partner, her friend, the man who had always covered her back, who had stood beside her when the walls closed in. Gone. Brutally taken. His body was riddled with bullet wounds, his face frozen in a mixture of shock and pain.

And she knew. Deep down, she knew. This was on her. All of it.

Flowers had tried to warn her. He told her what Porscha had said, the threats, the warnings. He had tried to make her see reason, but she hadn't wanted to hear it. All she could see was Porscha. All she wanted was Porscha. To Marlena, Porscha represented every piece of filth that had poisoned her city, every ghost that haunted her sleepless nights. She'd become obsessed. She ignored the danger, ignored her friend's pleas, and now? Now Flowers was dead. His babies were dead. Their blood stained her hands.

As Marlena got into her car, she gripped the steering wheel so tightly her knuckles went white. The tears streamed freely now, hot and bitter. She didn't bother wiping them away. The weight of guilt pressed on her chest like a boulder. She slammed the palm of her hand against the dashboard, over and over, until her skin bruised.

"Goddammit!" she roared, the sound ripping from her throat like an animal's cry.

The city outside blurred as she sped through the streets, headlights streaking past like ghosts. She didn't remember the drive home—only the endless replay of what she had seen. Flowers' face. His children's faces. The blood. The stillness. The finality of it.

When she pulled into her driveway, she sat there for a long time, staring at her front door. The house was dark. The house she had once considered her sanctuary now felt cold, empty. Slowly, she stepped out of the car, her legs weak, the weight of the night dragging at her every movement.

She unlocked the door, pushed it open, and took a single step inside.

Her foot slipped. Her body pitched forward, crashing hard to the floor. Pain shot through her elbow, her hip. Disoriented, she blinked, trying to understand what had just happened. The metallic smell hit her first—thick, coppery, unmistakable.

Blood.

Everywhere.

She pushed herself up, her hands sticky with it. Her heart pounded in her ears as she fumbled for the light switch. When the room illuminated, the sight that met her eyes made her stomach twist, bile rising in her throat.

Blood coated the floorboards, smeared across the walls, pooling beneath the furniture. And there—just to her left— lay the mutilated bodies of her two German Shepherds. Loyal, protective, beloved. Their heads had been severed cleanly, placed grotesquely atop their bodies as if on display. Their glassy eyes stared at nothing.

Marlena stumbled back, hand to her mouth, tears spilling fresh and hot down her cheeks. She wanted to scream but couldn't find the breath. She looked up, and that's when she saw it—scrawled across the wall in large, jagged letters, written in blood.

WALK AWAY NOW. THE ICE YOU ARE WALKING ON IS REAL THIN.

The words made her knees buckle. She clutched the edge of a table to stay upright, her mind reeling. That phrase…Flowers had told her. That's what Porscha had said to him. And before her, Detective Boatwright had gotten the same warning. She remembered Boatwright's face, pale and hollowed out by fear in those final days before she was gunned down. And now the message was here. In her home. In her blood-soaked sanctuary.

They had been in her house. They had slaughtered her animals. They had defiled her safe space. And they had done it to send a message.

Marlena stood there, shaking, breathing hard, staring at the writing as if it might change if she just blinked enough. But it didn't. The blood on the wall was as real as the blood on her hands. The reality was undeniable.

She had a choice. She could pick up her phone, call it in, and bring the department down on this. Bring in crime scene techs, detectives, reporters, the whole circus. Or…

Or she could do what she should have done from the start. Handle this herself.

No rules. No protocol. No red tape.

Just old school justice.

Her jaw clenched as the decision crystallized in her mind. Her eyes, so full of grief moments ago, now burned with cold fury. Porscha wanted a war? She was going to get one. And Marlena wasn't coming for her with a badge and a warrant this time.

She was coming for her with blood in her heart and vengeance in her hands.

Marlena moved through the house like a ghost, careful not to disturb the crime scene more than necessary. She stepped over the bodies of her dogs, whispering an apology she knew they couldn't hear. She went upstairs, stripped off her bloodstained clothes, and showered quickly, scrubbing herself raw, as if she could wash away the guilt. When she emerged, she was changed—not just outwardly, in clean jeans and a black leather jacket—but inside. The weight of guilt was still there, but it had been forged into something sharper, something that could cut.

She opened her closet, pulled out the lockbox she hadn't touched in years, and retrieved the contents. Her old service revolver, the one she kept as backup, a combat knife from her academy days, a worn, creased photo of herself and Flowers from when they'd made detective together. She stared at the picture, tracing his face with her thumb.

"I swear to you, I'll make this right," she whispered.

Marlena packed a small duffel with the essentials— ammo, gloves, burner phone, a map of the city with Porscha's known haunts circled in red. She knew she wouldn't sleep tonight. Wouldn't eat. Wouldn't stop. The hunt had begun, and she wouldn't stop until she stood over Porscha's body.

The streets seemed darker as she left the house, locking the door behind her out of habit though she knew it no longer mattered. The wind was cold, biting. It carried the sounds of the city—sirens in the distance, a dog barking, the hum of traffic. Life went on, oblivious to the war brewing in Marlena's heart.

As she drove, her mind raced. Every piece of intel, every whisper on the street, every file she'd ever pulled on Porscha played back in her head. She thought of the bodies left in Porscha's wake—the judge Trayvon had dumped in the lake, the execution of Sammy the Don, Lance murdered in his car, Jessica hanged in her own home, Boatwright assassinated at a funeral, Flowers and his babies slaughtered. The list went on and on.

And now it was personal. Too personal.

Marlena wasn't just chasing a criminal anymore. She was chasing the demon who had destroyed her and killed the people she was close to as well

"Thin ice?" she muttered, her voice low, dangerous. "You're the one who's about to fall through."

She parked her car in a dark alley, cut the engine, and sat in silence, watching the lights of Porscha's club in the distance. The place where so many deals had gone down, where so many bodies had fallen. She knew Porscha would feel untouchable there, surrounded by her guards, her soldiers, her empire. But Marlena didn't care.

Old school meant no rules. No waiting. No backup. Just action.

She stepped out of the car, duffel over her shoulder, revolver heavy at her side. She moved through the shadows like death itself, silent, unseen. The night air filled her lungs, sharpening her focus, feeding the fire Inside her.

It wasn't about the badge anymore. It wasn't about justice.

It was about vengeance.

And she would not stop until Porscha paid for every drop of blood she'd spilled. After two hours, just standing in the cut looking at Porscha's Club Mercedes, she made her way back to her car and just watched, eyes focused on the club and nothing else.

***

It was supposed to be just another night. The hum of bass from inside Porscha's club throbbed through the street, a heartbeat of sin, deals, and danger. The kind of night where empires grew and fell in whispers.

But not tonight.

Tonight, the storm had come for Trayvon.

Marlena Greaves sat behind the wheel of her unmarked car with her eyes locked on the black SUV pulling away from the club's back entrance. Her heart was pounding—but not with fear. With fury. With vengeance.

"There you are, motherfucker."

She grabbed her phone, dialing a number from memory. A voice answered on the first ring.

"Yo, Greaves."

"Follow that black SUV leaving Club Mercedes. I want it pulled over—clean. We're bringing him in."

"No warrant?"

"Fake one. Just do it. He's mine."

"Say less."

Marlena threw the car into gear, merging into the night behind her target.

The black SUV rolled through the city like it owned the night. But Greaves wasn't about to let it slip away. Not this time.

The black SUV was boxed in. Blue and red strobes flashed as Marlena's friend—another crooked badge—

waved a piece of paper that wouldn't hold up in any courtroom.

Trayvon stepped out, hands raised, a look of disgust on his face.

"The fuck is this?"

"Warrant," the cop smirked.

"For what?"

"You'll see soon enough."

Cuffs clicked onto Trayvon's wrists. He knew right then this wasn't official. This was personal.

***

They dragged him inside—filthy walls, broken glass crunching under boots. Marlena slammed him into a chair, chaining him down like an animal.

Trayvon spat blood onto the floor. "You don't know what you're doing, bitch."

"Oh, I know exactly what I'm doing," Marlena hissed, stepping close, revolver heavy in her hand.

She raised it—and cracked him across the face. The sound echoed, metal meeting bone.

Trayvon's head snapped to the side, blood pouring from his lip.

"That's for Flowers. For his kids. You remember them? The kids your daughter had snatched? The ones you helped her bury?"

"You don't know shit—"

She hit him again, harder.

"Don't lie to me! I'm done with the lies. You think Porscha can just take whatever she wants? Kill whoever she wants? You think I'm gonna sit back and cry while she walks free?"

Trayvon laughed, blood on his teeth. "You ain't ready for what's coming."

Marlena's eyes darkened. She turned to her partner. "Give me your phone."

Her fingers shook with rage as she scrolled through her contacts. Homeland Security. They'd been sniffing around Sanchez for years. Greaves had connections. She called the number they gave her, a line no cop was supposed to have.

It rang once, twice, three times.

Then, that voice. Calm. Deadly.

"Who is this?"

Marlena didn't hesitate.

"I have something you want. For a price."

Sanchez chuckled darkly. "And what do I want?"

"The man who tried to kill you. I know everything. Trayvon. He's mine now."

Silence on the line. Then, as if on cue, Sanchez's phone chimed with the picture Marlena's partner had just sent—the image of Trayvon tied down, face bloodied, defeated.

Sanchez stared at it. His lips curled into a grin.

"How much?"

"One million. Cash."

Sanchez studied the photo again. The man who'd dared to plot against him.

"Agreed. My men will be there in a few hours. I'll send the location."

Click.

Marlena lit a cigarette, staring at Trayvon like he was nothing.

"All that power. All that money. And look at you now. You're going to die like a rat, sold to the highest bidder."

Trayvon didn't answer. His breathing was ragged, but his eyes burned with hatred.

"Your daughter's next," Marlena whispered. "I'll see her empire burn."

***

Back at the club, Porscha was leaning over her office desk, going over plans for a shipment. Her phone rang—one of her drivers.

"Yeah?"

"Boss… Trayvon. They… they took him."

Porscha froze. "Who took him? Who the fuck—"

"The IA bitch. Greaves. She set him up. Fake warrant. Took him somewhere. I swear I didn't know—"

The driver's voice faded as Porscha's mind raced.

Then the second call came. No name. Just a number she didn't recognize.

"Hello?"

A voice she'd heard before—but only in whispered threats from the streets.

Sanchez.

"We need to talk. Or you can bury your father. The clock is ticking."

A picture followed. Trayvon. Tied down. Beaten. Bloodied.

Porscha stared at it. The club noise disappeared. The world disappeared. All that existed was that image.

Her father.

Her blood.

Her rage boiled over.

Porscha stood at the window of her office, the city spread out beneath her.

Her hands clenched into fists.

Her eyes burned holes in the night.

"This ends now," she whispered to the dark

Behind her, Paris, Corey, and Realz waited silently, knowing what that look meant.

War was coming.

The city spread out beneath Porscha like a graveyard of secrets, the lights flickering in the dark like dying souls. She stood at the window of her office, unmoving, the hum of the club below lost to the storm inside her mind. The music, the voices, the business of the night—it all faded beneath the sound of her heartbeat, loud and hollow in her chest.

In her hand, the phone still glowed with that picture. Trayvon. Tied down. Beaten. Bleeding. The man who had made her. The man who had taught her this life.

Her reflection stared back at her in the glass—eyes that looked dead, a face that no longer belonged to the girl she once was. Behind those eyes, she saw it all. Every step. Every sin.

The gun I pointed at so many people, she thought, her fingers trembling around the phone. *Now it's pointed at me.*

Her heart pounded against the weight of memory.

She was eighteen when she first killed and the world still seemed like it could offer something besides blood. But that night, down at the docks, when that rival crew cornered her, she had felt the cold steel of the pistol in her hand. She remembered how heavy it had been, how the metal seemed to burn against her skin. The man had stepped toward her, cocky, sure she wouldn't pull the trigger.

But she did.

The gunshot echoed through her soul as much as the night air. She watched him fall, watched the life drain from his eyes, those same eyes that stared at her like they couldn't believe what she'd done.

Trayvon had been there, just behind her, his voice low and proud.

"Good girl. That's how we survive."

And so, she survived.

Then came Boatwright. Detective Boatwright. The cop who wouldn't bend, wouldn't break. Porscha had tried everything from talking to her, threats, promises. But Boatwright had been stubborn, too stubborn. At Captain Lawson's funeral, Porscha gave the order. Corey on the motorcycle. Two shots to the head. No witnesses. No mercy.

Porscha wished she could have watched from the shadows as Boatwright's body crumpled beside her car. But it would have been too big of a risk. She said in a low tone, "You made me do that," she'd whispered.

But the truth was, she hadn't hesitated.

And the judge who just wouldn't give up had to die. Trayvon told her there was no other way. She could still see the body floating in the lake, the water dark and endless. She could picture Trayvon's face as he stood on the shore, water dripping from his hands, his eyes as empty as the sky above.

"Sometimes you gotta feed the fish," he'd said.

Porscha had laughed then. Laughed at death like it was nothing.

Jessica. That one haunted her some nights. The smell of that house. The creak of the rope. Jessica's body swaying gently, face twisted in fear and regret. Trayvon's work. His message to anyone thinking of betrayal.

Porscha hadn't stopped him. She hadn't even flinched.

And Sammy. Sammy the Don. The man who'd called her a child, a girl playing a man's game. He'd found out the hard way. Paris, Corey, Realz—they'd made sure of that. She could still see Sammy's eyes when he realized the end had come. When he realized it was her who'd signed his death.

The parking lot. Lance. The blood on the windshield. The way his head snapped back when the bullets hit. Pauly didn't think she would find out. Pauly thought he was untouchable. Thought he could run his mouth and still walk around like nothing would happen now he's dead. A life for a life.

Pauly's nephew. The boy who vanished. Lucchese's order, Donnie's hands—but Porscha wanted more than just Pauly dead and Lucchese knew this. That's why he had his nephew killed. No body. No trace. Just a mother's tears, a sister's screams, a family destroyed.

And now?

Now the gun was turned on her.

Porscha pressed her forehead to the glass, the coolness of it grounding her as the storm inside threatened to consume her.

I did this. We did this.

Every choice. Every body. Every night she'd stood at this window thinking she was on top. It had all led here. To a phone call from Sanchez. To a picture of her father, chained and broken.

Her fingers tightened on the phone. The rage boiled beneath her skin, but so did the fear. The kind of fear that came when the game turned against you.

Behind her, Paris and Corey waited. Silent. Watching. Knowing what that look meant.

But Porscha couldn't speak. Couldn't move.

She saw them all. Boatwright. Jessica. Sammy. Lance. Faces of the dead, staring at her from the shadows of her mind. The gunshots. The screams. The silence after.

She tasted the smoke of a hundred gunfights. Smelled the gasoline of burning cars. Felt the weight of the pistol in her hand, the night it all began.

I was just a girl.

Now?

Now I'm this.

Sanchez's voice echoed inside her.

"We need to talk. Or you can bury your father."

Her own voice rose to meet it.

"This ends now."

But did it? Could it?

The empire she'd built on blood, on fear, on death—was it crumbling beneath her feet? Or was this just another war to win?

She didn't know. All she knew was that the clock was ticking. And it was ticking fast.

To be continued

Lock Down Publications and Ca$h Presents
Assisted Publishing Packages

Due to an increase in the price of services we have increased our prices. The prices below reflect the price increase as of 11/1/24.

BASIC PACKAGE **$699** Editing Cover Design Formatting	UPGRADED PACKAGE **$1000** Typing Editing Cover Design Formatting Upload eBooks to Amazon Upload Paperback to Amazon
ADVANCE PACKAGE **$1,400** Typing Editing (line editing/content) Cover Design Formatting Copyright Registration Proofreading Upload eBooks to Amazon Upload Paperback to Amazon	LDP SUPREME PACKAGE **$1,700** Typing Editing (line editing/content) Cover Design Formatting Copyright Registration Proofreading Set up Amazon Account Upload eBooks to Amazon Upload Paperback to Amazon Advertise on LDP's Amazon and Facebook Page

***

Other services available upon request.
Additional charges may apply

Lock Down Publications
P.O. Box 944
Stockbridge, GA 30281-9998
Phone: 470 303-9761
Email: lockdownpublications@gmail.com

Submission Guideline

Submit the first three chapters of your completed manuscript to ldpsubmissions@gmail.com. In the subject line add **Your Book's Title**. The manuscript must be in a Word Doc file and sent as an attachment. Document should be in Times New Roman, double spaced, and in size 12 font. Also, provide your synopsis and full contact information. If sending multiple submissions, they must each be in a separate email.

Have a story but no way to send it electronically? You can still submit to LDP/Ca$h Presents. Send in the first three chapters, written or typed, of your completed manuscript to:

LDP: Submissions Dept
P.O. Box 944
Stockbridge, GA 30281-9998

DO NOT send original manuscript. Must be a duplicate. Provide your synopsis and a cover letter containing your full contact information.

Thanks for considering LDP and Ca$h Presents.

NEW RELEASES

BLOODLINE OF A SAVAGE 1-3
THESE VICIOUS STREETS 1-3
RELENTLESS GOON 1-3
BY PRINCE A. TAUHID

THE BUTTERFLY MAFIA 1-3
BY FUMIYA PAYNE

A THUG'S STREET PRINCESS 1&2
BY MEESHA

CITY OF SMOKE 3
BY MOLOTTI

GET IT IN SLUGS 1 &2
BY B. STALL

STANDING ON HER BUSINESS 1&2
BY DG SANTANA

STEPPERS 1,2&3
THE REAL BADDIES OF CHI-RAQ
BY KING RIO

THE LANE 1&2
BY KEN-KEN SPENCE

THUG OF SPADES 1&2
LOVE IN THE TRENCHES 2
CORNER BOYS
BY COREY ROBINSON

TIL DEATH 3
BY ARYANNA

THE DAUGHTER OF A CARTEL BOSS 2

THE BIRTH OF A GANGSTER 4
BY DELMONT PLAYER

PRODUCT OF THE STREETS 1-3
BY DEMOND "MONEY" ANDERSON

NO TIME FOR ERROR
BY KEESE

MONEY HUNGRY DEMONS 1-2
BY TRANAY ADAMS

HUB CITY MENACE 1-3
BY J. WHITE

A THUGGISH PASSION 1&2
LAND OF DA HOOLIGANZ 1-4
KILLAZ ON STANDBY 1&2
BY IRA B.

FO'EVA ROLLIN 1&2
BY ASSA RAYMOND BAKER

THE LEVEL UP 1&3
BY LUXURY KING

Coming Soon from Lock Down Publications/Ca$h Presents

IF YOU CROSS ME ONCE 6
ANGEL V
By Anthony Fields

A THUGS STREET PRINCESS 3
By Meesha

CORNER BOYS 2
By Corey Robinson

THA TAKEOVER
By Keith Chandler

BETRAYAL OF A G 2
By Ray Vinci

SAVAGE FAMILY EMPIRE 1&2
SOULLESS GOON 1,2&3
THE DIRTY SIDE OF MONEY 1,2&3
By Prince

FOR MY ENEMY'S SAKE
AMBITIONS OF A SLIDER
FRESH OFF DA PORCH
By IRA B.

THE TRUCKLOAD 1-4
TIPPIN' THE SCALES 1-3
BAD BITCHES WIT GUNZ 3
PROBLEM SOLVED 2
By Christopher "Diesel" Hornezes

Available Now

RESTRAINING ORDER 1 & 2
By **CA$H & Coffee**

LOVE KNOWS NO BOUNDARIES 1-3
By **Coffee**

RAISED AS A GOON I, II, III & IV
BRED BY THE SLUMS I, II, III
BLAST FOR ME I & II
ROTTEN TO THE CORE I II III
A BRONX TALE I, II, III
DUFFLE BAG CARTEL I II III IV V VI
HEARTLESS GOON I II III IV V
A SAVAGE DOPEBOY I II
DRUG LORDS I II III
CUTTHROAT MAFIA I II
KING OF THE TRENCHES
By **Ghost**

LAY IT DOWN I & II
LAST OF A DYING BREED I II
BLOOD STAINS OF A SHOTTA I & II III
By **Jamaica**

LOYAL TO THE GAME I II III
LIFE OF SIN I, II III
By **TJ & Jelissa**

IF LOVING HIM IS WRONG…I & II
LOVE ME EVEN WHEN IT HURTS I II III
By **Jelissa**

PUSH IT TO THE LIMIT
By **Bre' Hayes**

SAYNOMORE

BLOODY COMMAS I & II
SKI MASK CARTEL I, II & III
KING OF NEW YORK I II, III IV V
RISE TO POWER I II III
COKE KINGS I II III IV V
BORN HEARTLESS I II III IV
KING OF THE TRAP I II
By **T.J. Edwards**

WHEN THE STREETS CLAP BACK I & II III
THE HEART OF A SAVAGE I II III IV
MONEY MAFIA I II
LOYAL TO THE SOIL I II III
By **Jibril Williams**

A DISTINGUISHED THUG STOLE MY HEART I II & III
LOVE SHOULDN'T HURT I II III IV
RENEGADE BOYS 1-4
PAID IN KARMA 1-3
SAVAGE STORMS 1-3
AN UNFORESEEN LOVE 1-3
BABY, I'M WINTERTIME COLD 1-3
A THUG'S STREET PRINCESS 1&2
By **Meesha**

A GANGSTER'S CODE 1-3
A GANGSTER'S SYN 1-3
THE SAVAGE LIFE 1-3
CHAINED TO THE STREETS 1-3
BLOOD ON THE MONEY 1-3
A GANGSTA'S PAIN 1-3
BEAUTIFUL LIES AND UGLY TRUTHS
CHURCH IN THESE STREETS
By **J-Blunt**

CUM FOR ME 1-8
An LDP Erotica Collaboration

THE DAUGHTER OF A CARTEL BOSS 2

BLOOD OF A BOSS 1-5
SHADOWS OF THE GAME
TRAP BASTARD
By **Askari**

THE STREETS BLEED MURDER 1-3
THE HEART OF A GANGSTA 1-3
By **Jerry Jackson**

WHEN A GOOD GIRL GOES BAD
By **Adrienne**

THE COST OF LOYALTY 1-3
By **Kweli**

BRIDE OF A HUSTLA 1-3
THE FETTI GIRLS 1-3
CORRUPTED BY A GANGSTA 1-4
BLINDED BY HIS LOVE
THE PRICE YOU PAY FOR LOVE 1-3
DOPE GIRL MAGIC 1-3
By **Destiny Skai**

A KINGPIN'S AMBITION
A KINGPIN'S AMBITION II
I MURDER FOR THE DOUGH
By **Ambitious**

TRUE SAVAGE 1-7
DOPE BOY MAGIC 1-3
MIDNIGHT CARTEL 1-3
CITY OF KINGZ 1&2
NIGHTMARE ON SILENT AVE
THE PLUG OF LIL MEXICO 1&2
CLASSIC CITY
By **Chris Green**

SAYNOMORE

A GANGSTER'S REVENGE 1-4
THE BOSS MAN'S DAUGHTERS 1-5
A SAVAGE LOVE 1&2
BAE BELONGS TO ME 1&2
A HUSTLER'S DECEIT 1-3
WHAT BAD BITCHES DO 1-3
SOUL OF A MONSTER 1-3
KILL ZONE
A DOPE BOY'S QUEEN 1-3
TIL DEATH 1-3
IMMA DIE BOUT MINE 1-6
DYING FOR LIKES
By **Aryanna**

A DOPEBOY'S PRAYER
By **Eddie "Wolf" Lee**

THE KING CARTEL 1-3
By **Frank Gresham**

THESE NIGGAS AIN'T LOYAL 1-3
By **Nikki Tee**

GANGSTA SHYT 1-3
By **CATO**

THE ULTIMATE BETRAYAL
By **Phoenix**

BOSS'N UP 1-3
By **Royal Nicole**

I LOVE YOU TO DEATH
By **Destiny J**

I RIDE FOR MY HITTA
I STILL RIDE FOR MY HITTA
By **Misty Holt**

THE DAUGHTER OF A CARTEL BOSS 2

LOVE & CHASIN' PAPER
By **Qay Crockett**

TO DIE IN VAIN
SINS OF A HUSTLA
By **ASAD**

BROOKLYN HUSTLAZ
By **Boogsy Morina**

BROOKLYN ON LOCK 1 & 2
By **Sonovia**

GANGSTA CITY
By **Teddy Duke**

A DRUG KING AND HIS DIAMOND 1-3
A DOPEMAN'S RICHES
HER MAN, MINE'S TOO 1&2
CASH MONEY HO'S
THE WIFEY I USED TO BE 1&2
PRETTY GIRLS DO NASTY THINGS
By **Nicole Goosby**

LIPSTICK KILLAH 1-3
CRIME OF PASSION 1-3
FRIEND OR FOE 1-3
By **Mimi**

TRAPHOUSE KING 1-3
KINGPIN KILLAZ 1-3
STREET KINGS 1&2
PAID IN BLOOD 1&2
CARTEL KILLAZ 1-3
DOPE GODS 1&2
By **Hood Rich**

THE STREETS ARE CALLING
By **Duquie Wilson**

SAYNOMORE

STEADY MOBBN' 1-3
THE STREETS STAINED MY SOUL 1-3
By **Marcellus Allen**

WHO SHOT YA 1-3
SON OF A DOPE FIEND 1-4
HEAVEN GOT A GHETTO 1&2
SKI MASK MONEY 1&2
By **Renta**

GORILLAZ IN THE BAY 1-4
TEARS OF A GANGSTA 1/&2
3X KRAZY 1&2
STRAIGHT BEAST MODE 1&2
By **DE'KARI**

TRIGGADALE 1-3
MURDA WAS THE CASE 1-3
By **Elijah R. Freeman**

SLAUGHTER GANG 1-3
RUTHLESS HEART 1-3
By **Willie Slaughter**

GOD BLESS THE TRAPPERS 1-3
THESE SCANDALOUS STREETS 1-3
FEAR MY GANGSTA 1-5
THESE STREETS DON'T LOVE NOBODY 1-2
BURY ME A G 1-5
A GANGSTA'S EMPIRE 1-4
THE DOPEMAN'S BODYGAURD 1&2
THE REALEST KILLAZ 1-3
THE LAST OF THE OGS 1-3
By **Tranay Adams**

MARRIED TO A BOSS 1-3
By **Destiny Skai & Chris Green**

THE DAUGHTER OF A CARTEL BOSS 2

KINGZ OF THE GAME 1-7
CRIME BOSS 1-4
By **Playa Ray**

FUK SHYT
By **Blakk Diamond**

DON'T F#CK WITH MY HEART 1&2
By **Linnea**

ADDICTED TO THE DRAMA 1-3
IN THE ARM OF HIS BOSS
By **Jamila**

LOYALTY AIN'T PROMISED 1&2
By **Keith Williams**

YAYO 1-4
A SHOOTER'S AMBITION 1&2
BRED IN THE GAME
By **S. Allen**

TRAP GOD 1-3
RICH $AVAGE 1-3
MONEY IN THE GRAVE 1-3
CARTEL MONEY 1&2
By **Martell Troublesome Bolden**

FOREVER GANGSTA 1&2
GLOCKS ON SATIN SHEETS 1&2
By **Adrian Dulan**

TOE TAGZ 1-4
LEVELS TO THIS SHYT 1&2
IT'S JUST ME AND YOU
By **Ah'Million**

SAYNOMORE

KINGPIN DREAMS 1-3
RAN OFF ON DA PLUG
By **Paper Boi Rari**

THE STREETS MADE ME 1-3
By **Larry D. Wright**

CONFESSIONS OF A GANGSTA 1-4
CONFESSIONS OF A JACKBOY 1-3
CONFESSIONS OF A HITMAN
CONFESSIONS OF A DOPE BOY
By **Nicholas Lock**

I'M NOTHING WITHOUT HIS LOVE
SINS OF A THUG
TO THE THUG I LOVED BEFORE
A GANGSTA SAVED XMAS
IN A HUSTLER I TRUST
By **Monet Dragun**

QUIET MONEY 1-3
THUG LIFE 1-3
EXTENDED CLIP 1&2
A GANGSTA'S PARADISE
By **Trai'Quan**

CAUGHT UP IN THE LIFE 1-3
THE STREETS NEVER LET GO 1-3
By **Robert Baptiste**

NEW TO THE GAME 1-3
MONEY, MURDER & MEMORIES 1-3
By **Malik D. Rice**

CREAM 2-3
THE STREETS WILL TALK
By **Yolanda Moore**

THE DAUGHTER OF A CARTEL BOSS 2

THE STREETS WILL NEVER CLOSE 1-3
By **K'ajji**

LIFE OF A SAVAGE 1-4
A GANGSTA'S QUR'AN 1-4
MURDA SEASON 1-3
GANGLAND CARTEL 1-3
CHI'RAQ GANGSTAS 1-4
KILLERS ON ELM STREET 1-3
JACK BOYZ N DA BRONX 1-3
A DOPEBOY'S DREAM 1-3
JACK BOYS VS DOPE BOYS 1-3
COKE GIRLZ
COKE BOYS
SOSA GANG 1&2
BRONX SAVAGES
BODYMORE KINGPINS
BLOOD OF A GOON
By **Romell Tukes**

CONCRETE KILLA 1-3
VICIOUS LOYALTY 1-3
BLOODY MONEY BAGS
By **Kingpen**

THE ULTIMATE SACRIFICE 1-6
KHADIFI
IF YOU CROSS ME ONCE 1-3
ANGEL 1-4
IN THE BLINK OF AN EYE
By **Anthony Fields**

THE LIFE OF A HOOD STAR
By **Ca$h & Rashia Wilson**

NIGHTMARES OF A HUSTLA 1-3
BLOOD AND GAMES 1&2
By **King Dream**

SAYNOMORE

GHOST MOB
By **Stilloan Robinson**

HARD AND RUTHLESS 1&2
MOB TOWN 251
THE BILLIONAIRE BENTLEYS 1-3
REAL G'S MOVE IN SILENCE
By **Von Diesel**

MOB TIES 1-7
SOUL OF A HUSTLER, HEART OF A KILLER 1-3
GORILLAZ IN THE TRENCHES
OOPS CRY TOO 1&2
THE DAUGHTER OF A CARTEL BOSS
By **SayNoMore**

BODYMORE MURDERLAND 1-3
THE BIRTH OF A GANGSTER 1-4
By **Delmont Player**

FOR THE LOVE OF A BOSS 1&2
By **C. D. Blue**

KILLA KOUNTY 1-5
TENDER
By **Khufu**

MOBBED UP 1-4
THE BRICK MAN 1-5
THE COCAINE PRINCESS 1-10
STEPPERS 1-3
SUPER GREMLIN 1-4
A GANGSTA'S SON
By **King Rio**

MONEY GAME 1&2
By **Smoove Dolla**

THE DAUGHTER OF A CARTEL BOSS 2

A GANGSTA'S KARMA 1-5
By **FLAME**

KING OF THE TRENCHES 1-3
By **GHOST & TRANAY ADAMS**

BAD BITCHES WIT GUNZ 1&2
PROBLEM SOLVED
By **"Christopher Diesel" Hornezes**

QUEEN OF THE ZOO 1&2
By **Black Migo**

GRIMEY WAYS 1-3
BETRAYAL OF A G
By **Ray Vinci**

XMAS WITH AN ATL SHOOTER
By **Ca$h & Destiny Skai**

KING KILLA 1&2
By **Vincent "Vitto" Holloway**

BETRAYAL OF A THUG 1&2
By **Fre$h**

COUNTDOWN OF A KILLA 1&2
SEX, MURDER AND GOD 1&2
GUNS DOWN, BOTTOMS UP 1&2
By Lo-Life

THE MURDER QUEENS 1-7
By **Michael Gallon**

FOR THE LOVE OF BLOOD 1-4
By **Jamel Mitchell**

SAYNOMORE

HOOD CONSIGLIERE 1&2
NO TIME FOR ERROR
By **Keese**

PROTÉGÉ OF A LEGEND 1,2&3
LOVE IN THE TRENCHES 1&2
By **Corey Robinson**

THE PLUG'S RUTHLESS DAUGHTER 1&2
By **Tony Daniels**

BORN IN THE GRAVE 1-3
CRIME PAYS
By **Self Made Tay**

MOAN IN MY MOUTH
By **XTASY**

TORN BETWEEN A GANGSTER AND A GENTLEMAN
By **J-BLUNT & Miss Kim**

LOYALTY IS EVERYTHING 1-3
CITY OF SMOKE 1-3
By **Molotti**

HERE TODAY GONE TOMORROW 1&2
By **Fly Rock**

WOMEN LIE MEN LIE 1-4
FIFTY SHADES OF SNOW 1-3
STACK BEFORE YOU SPLURGE
GIRLS FALL LIKE DOMINOES
NAÏVE TO THE STREETS
By **ROY MILLIGAN**

PILLOW PRINCESS
By **S. Hawkins**

THE DAUGHTER OF A CARTEL BOSS 2

THE BUTTERFLY MAFIA 1-3
SALUTE MY SAVAGERY 1&2
By **Fumiya Payne**

THE LANE 1&2
By Ken-Ken Spence

THE PUSSY TRAP 1-5
By **Nene Capri**

DIRTY DNA
By **Blaque**

SANCTIFIED AND HORNY
by **XTASY**

BOOKS BY LDP'S CEO, CA$H

TRUST IN NO MAN
TRUST IN NO MAN 2
TRUST IN NO MAN 3
BONDED BY BLOOD
SHORTY GOT A THUG
THUGS CRY
THUGS CRY 2
THUGS CRY 3
TRUST NO BITCH
TRUST NO BITCH 2
TRUST NO BITCH 3
TIL MY CASKET DROPS
RESTRAINING ORDER
RESTRAINING ORDER 2
IN LOVE WITH A CONVICT
LIFE OF A HOOD STAR
XMAS WITH AN ATL SHOOTER

www.ingramcontent.com/pod-product-compliance
Lightning Source LLC
Chambersburg PA
CBHW071206260626
47162CB00003B/1187

* 9 7 8 1 9 6 5 4 4 8 9 5 3 *